BOY WITH A PACK

BOY WITH A PACK

by STEPHEN W. MEADER

ILLUSTRATED BY EDWARD SHENTON

SOUTHERN SKIES
LITTLE ROCK, ARKANSAS
www.southernskies.com

Dedication

The republication of this book is dedicated with love to the memory of Joseph Morrow Sherman by his best boyhood friend, Jerry Atchley, who walked many miles with him.

BOY WITH A PACK

CHAPTER

IT was still dark when Bill Crawford crawled out of his cot under the steep slope of the rafters. Cold, too. He was shivering as he whipped on his wool undershirt and struggled into his homespun breeches. A candle stood on a box by the head of the cot but there was no use trying to

ONE

light it with flint and steel. He fumbled under the bed and found his socks and the stiff new boots of heavy cowhide. Once he had stamped his feet into them he felt warmer and more awake.

Groping along the narrow attic, he reached the one small window in the gable end and peered out.

The sky showed a few stars, fading now as the east brightened. The shaggy shoulders of Mt. Monad·nock cut a rugged silhouette against the dawn. It was going to be clear, Bill decided. A cold, clear April day.

He pulled a tow shirt over his head and buckled his belt. Below in the house the family was stirring and as the boy clumped down the stairs he heard the tolling of the mill bell across the river. That was the five-thirty warning bell. At six it would be ringing again as the last workers hastened through the doors and the looms began to clack.

Bill's brother Wash—short for Washington—was bent above the tin basin, spluttering and blowing as he scrubbed the sleep out of his eyes with pump-water. By the hearth Wash's young wife stirred the pot of "rye-and-injun" mush that would be their breakfast. She was a pale, tired-looking girl with dark eyes that seemed too big for her thin face.

"Morning, Bill," she murmured, and Wash, groping for the huck towel, turned to blink at his brother from under dripping brows.

"You're up early," he grunted. Then, remembering, "Oh—this is the day you start?"

Bill nodded. "Hope to be 'most to the Connecticut River by nightfall," he answered with a briskness he did not feel.

"Hmm. Your pack all ready?"

" 'Twill be, soon as I fix the straps. All it needs is a couple more holes, so I can carry the load higher on my back."

"Well," the older brother yawned, "I've still got no patience with the idea. A job's a job, 'specially in these hard times. No use my arguing though, I guess, if you're bound to go. You take after Ma's folks, an' they was always pigheaded."

Bill let the remark pass and sat down in his place at the deal table. Jenny was ladling out the mush into bowls. It had a steamy, pleasant smell that became downright tempting when the maple 'lasses was poured over it. The boy stirred vigorously and blew on the first spoonful but it was still too hot to eat.

Wash looked at him with a half-humorous twinkle in his eye. "Don't let them Injuns scalp you," he said, "when you get out there in the wilderness."

Jenny gave a frightened gasp and her husband

patted her arm. "I was only foolin'," he explained. "Plenty of other peddlers have gone from round here, an' they generally get back from the western country with their hair on."

"Shucks," Bill laughed. "I won't likely even see an Injun. They tell me Ohio's so settled up now the farms and towns are thicker'n they are here in New Hampshire."

"Ohio!" Jenny sighed. "My, it seems like the other side o' the world when you talk about goin' there. And you're such a youngster, Billy!"

"Seventeen isn't so young," Bill bristled. "Grandad Crawford was fighting the red-coats when he was a year younger. Besides, I'm big enough to pass for a man. Remember how Mr. Jenness, at the bank, asked me if I voted for Van Buren last fall?"

"Yeah?" Wash grinned. "What did you tell him?"

"I told him if I'd been votin' it would be for Dan'l Webster—not for any 'York State Dutchman."

"You'd better learn to watch that Whig tongue when you get on west," Wash warned him. "Plenty o' Van Buren men where you're goin', I reckon."

He pushed back his empty bowl and stood up, stretching. " 'Bout time to go to work," he grumbled. "Well, I'll wish you luck, boy. I guess you're Yankee enough not to let 'em cheat you. We'll be lookin' for you back before frost."

They shook hands soberly. Wash kissed his wife and went to the door. With his thumb on the latch he turned to face his brother again. "Forget what I said," he smiled wryly. "Guess I'd do the same in your place. It takes real grit to tackle a trip like that, an' you've got plenty of it."

With that he was gone. They heard him hurrying down the path as the first slow strokes of the six o'clock bell echoed in the little valley.

"Better eat some more," Jenny said. "Goodness knows how you'll get fed, the next few months."

She helped him to another bowl of mush and pushed the 'lasses jug toward him. "You know," she said, "Wash really thinks a heap of you, Bill. We're goin' to miss you."

The boy finished his breakfast in silence. He hated to get up from the table because it seemed to bring the moment of departure so much nearer. He had never been thirty miles from Fairfield in his life—never sold anything. And here he was, about to set out with a peddler's pack, bound for a vague destination many hundreds of miles away. For a moment he wished he had taken the job in the mill—the safe, unadventurous job, at two certain dollars a week. Then he shook himself angrily and shoved back his stool.

"The sun's up, Jenny," he remarked, with businesslike cheerfulness. "I'll have to be taking the road."

He cut two extra holes in the stout leather straps that were to hold the pack on his shoulders. Then he set the tin trunk on the table and took a last careful look at its contents. The spools of cotton thread, the needles and pins, the scissors and thimbles; the ear-rings and beads; the pocket combs and little mirrors; the bits of lace and ribbon; the jew's-harps and pocket-knives—all the varied knickknacks he had purchased were packed in their separate compartments. Forty dollars' worth of merchandise! The savings of two years of wood-chopping, berry-picking and odd farm jobs —all risked on this crazy venture of his.

He drew a deep breath and fastened the cover

firmly. The big wood-box by the fireplace was empty, he saw. Two trips to the woodpile behind the house filled it to the brim and his last chore was done. There was nothing to keep him any longer.

He put his arms through the pack-straps, and hunched his shoulders to bring the trunk comfortably into place. The oilskin-covered bundle that held his blanket, spare socks and shirts, and small utensils was slipped under the straps on top of the trunk. As he turned to go Jenny put a package in his hand.

"It's some lunch, Billy," she said. "Not much, but at least I'll know you aren't goin' hungry for this one day. Good-by and good luck."

.   .   .   .

Outside, the sharp spring air tingled in his lungs. He stepped out with a long stride, his heavy boots ringing on the stony path. Slant beams of sunlight came over the eastern hill and touched the willows by the river with a haze of greenish gold. Somewhere in the bare trees a songsparrow was singing.

The road led through a covered bridge that crossed the river just above the mill. As he passed the many-windowed stone building he could hear the splash of the big waterwheels and the endless clatter of the looms. A hundred spinners and weavers toiled behind those walls twelve hours a day, making the Fairfield flannel that was famous through all New England. At one of the card-room windows Bill caught a glimpse of a lint-covered figure waving at him. It was Wash, seeing him off on his journey.

He climbed the westward hill and went on without looking back. The pack still felt light and the winding road was an invitation. He tramped along at a steady pace, his mind on the leagues ahead. A dozen miles to the big town of Keene, and twenty more before he reached the river. Then the Vermont hills to cross, and the whole vast length of New York State. He tried to picture the wall map that had hung in the one-room schoolhouse. New York, he remembered, was pinkish and Ohio was yellow. But wasn't there a small green section of Pennsylvania separating them, somewhere along the Lake Erie shore? A fine thing it would be if he went right through a state without knowing it!

He was well across the next valley now and starting to climb the hill on the other side. The sun grew hot as it rose in the sky. He felt the sweat starting on his forehead and took off his hat while he toiled upward. The new boots were heavy and hard to his feet, and the forty-pound pack tugged at its straps and cut into his shoulders. Bill made his way to a rambling stone wall beside the road and rested the trunk upon it while he mopped his face. He grinned as he thought how he had looked forward to this journey—the gay adventure of tramping the highways—seeking his fortune in far-off places. Here he was, six miles from home and tired already.

He had taken up his load again and was nearly at the top of the hill when he heard the clink of horseshoes on the slope behind him. A pair of sturdy, quick-stepping Morgans, hitched to a light wagon, pulled up abreast.

"Hi, me lad!" a loud voice called. "Would ye be wantin' a lift now?"

Bill turned and saw a short red-faced man smiling down at him.

"If you're going toward Keene, I'd be mighty grateful," he answered.

"Keene, is it? Sure an' I'm goin' right into the place! Sling yer pack behind the seat here, an' hop up," urged the driver.

In another moment Bill had climbed in over the wheel and the eager horses were on their way. The stocky little Irishman gave him a comical glance.

"A peddler y'are, from the looks of yer pack," he winked. "I'm a trader meself of a sort. John O'Hanlon's me name—cattle dealer, from over Jaffrey way. Are ye travelin' far from home?"

"Not far—yet," Bill laughed. "I live in Fairfield. Just started this morning."

Under the friendly questioning of the Irishman he told the whole story. "My brother's a wool-carder in the mill," he explained. "I've lived with him since Father died. This spring he tried to get a job for me, but times are hard and all they needed was a sweeper-boy at two dollars a week. Maybe if I'd been sensible I'd have taken it."

He paused, hunting for words to express himself. "I—well, I just didn't want to be shut up in there," he said. "It's gloomy in the mill, and dusty, and the hands don't see much daylight. They're hard at it from sunup till dark. I'm sort o' wild, I guess. I like it better outdoors. I tried the farms around, but nobody needed any help and money's so scarce they couldn't pay for it if they did. Anyhow, I took everything I'd saved and put it into notions and gimcracks, and now I'm heading for Ohio."

O'Hanlon chuckled. "I know," he said. "I had itchin' feet meself when I was a b'y. So ye're goin' to get rich, eh?"

"I wouldn't say that," Bill replied, reddening. "Don't know as I'll even make a good peddler. But at least I'll try and make my living and get a look at the westward country."

The matched Morgans trotted fast when they got on level ground, and they swung into the wide main street of Keene before ten o'clock. The Irishman pulled up in front of the town's principal tavern and helped Bill sling the pack on his shoulders.

"Luck go wid ye, lad," he told him at parting. "May ye come back wid yer trunk full o' siller an' ridin' a fine tall horse!"

Bill thanked him and started off down the street. The ride had rested him and now that he had passed the first milestone in his journey he began to feel like an old traveler.

Out in the fields beyond the town there were

farmers plowing. The big, patient, red-and-white oxen bowed forward under their yokes, pulling with a slow heave that never hurried, never stopped. Behind the plowmen, straddling their furrows, the brown earth lay in a clean curve, turned to the sun. And robins and flickers followed their progress, feasting on such morsels as were flung up by the plowshares.

Bill whistled as he tramped along, glad of the spring day. It was a lucky thing, he decided, that he had waited until after mud-time. The road was dry now, with loose dust that whitened his boots, but he could see from the hardened ruts what it must have been like when the frost was coming out of the ground.

At noon he took off his pack and sat down by the edge of a brook under some pines to eat his lunch. In the packet Jenny had given him there were half a loaf of bread, a wedge of cheese, three doughnuts and some home-made pickles. He ate sparingly, washed his food down with a drink of cold water from the brook, and wrapped what was left in the paper again. It was just as well, he thought, to have some rations in reserve.

There were hurrying clouds in the upper sky when he came over the next rise. Ahead of him their shadows dappled the green and brown of the broad countryside with moving patches of darker gray. "Showers," he thought, as he trudged forward. "Well, it's April. They're to be expected."

The rain held off through most of the afternoon and he had put a dozen miles more behind him when the first big drops came down. For twenty minutes the rain fell in a drenching torrent. Then the setting sun peeped through a rift of cloud and in a moment the shower was over. Bill had not tried to find shelter but had plugged along through the downpour. His stout jacket had shed most of the rain and his drooping hat had kept the water out of his collar. Still his clothes felt heavy and damp.

Going down the next slope his boots slithered in wet, slippery clay. For a few seconds he struggled to hold his footing. The weight of the pack unbalanced him and he had to wave his arms wildly to stay upright. At last he got one foot on the grass at the roadside and stood there panting, wet and tired.

He had lived in that part of the country long enough to know that where there was clay there was usually brick-making. The pungent smell of hardwood smoke that now drifted up the hill to him added to his certainty, and he was not surprised when he came to a rutted wheel track leading into the alder scrub, a short distance farther on.

The clouds were closing in black again and night would be falling soon. He had no idea how far it might be to the next village or farmhouse. After a moment's hesitation he turned to the right and followed the path.

A heavy silence hung over the thicket, broken only by the sounds of Bill's progress. He stumbled in the increasing darkness, and the alder shoots whipped his face and outstretched hands. The distance he had to traverse could not have been more than two hundred yards but his journey seemed endless. Once or twice he was tempted to turn back. Then the branches thinned ahead of him and he stepped out at the edge of a clearing.

As he had expected, the place was a brickyard. Sand and clay pits had been dug out of the hillside. There was the level drying floor with rows of gray bricks, molded and set to dry. There was the mixer, with its crude log arm and the deep-trampled circle around it where the horse had walked to turn the shaft. And beyond stood the kiln. It was a crude structure of bricks, built up like a house, with a sagging board roof over it. Along the bottom on either side ran a row of oven-openings shaped like little Gothic arches. And cordwood was stacked in ragged piles under the sloping extension of the roof.

Bill crossed the drying-yard and went toward the kiln. There were no brick-makers in sight. They must have quit work for the day. But he was sure to find someone tending the fires. Under the lean-to at the side of the kiln a ruddy glow came from the arched openings. The warmth of the red embers felt pleasant in the dampness and chill of evening. Bill went all the way around the structure without encountering anybody.

Puzzled, he stood by the mixer and looked about him. "Hello!" he shouted, and then, as loudly as he could, "Hello, the yard!"

There was no answer but the dreary drip of moisture from the eaves.

CHAPTER

BILL set down his pack in a dry place under the overhang of the kiln roof. For a moment he felt light and giddy with the weight gone from his shoulders. It was as if he were walking on tiptoe. He shouted once more and stood listening before he set out across the shadowy yard.

TWO

There was still light enough for him to see where he was going. He made his way between the rows of raw brick and reached the clay pit at the farther end of the clearing. Then, swinging to the left, he made a circuit along the edge of the woods. After going perhaps twenty paces he felt hard-packed ground under his feet and saw a path leading into the brush. Beyond it was the squat, dark outline of a building.

"That's it," he thought. "The bunk-house. Funny there's no light, though. Suppose they're all asleep?"

He went cautiously up the path, expecting to knock on the door. But when he reached it, the door stood open. Inside all was silent. A few burned-out coals in the fireplace gave the only light.

Bill hesitated on the threshold, struggling with a feeling that something was wrong. His voice shook a little when he finally spoke. "Is anybody here?" he asked.

The stillness was unbroken. Nervously the boy took a stump of candle from his pocket and crossed to the hearth. There was enough heat in the coals to light the wick. He nursed the little yellow flame behind his hand and looked around the shadowy room.

Something had happened here that he could not understand. Empty tin plates and mugs lay in confusion on the long, greasy table. One of the benches was overturned and the other jerked askew. Dirty clothes drooped haphazard from the edges of the dozen bunks that lined the walls. And on the crane above the dying fire a big black kettle hung from its hook, its sooty sides still warm. When Bill lifted the lid he saw an unsavory mess inside—a stew that might have been intended for the brick-makers' supper.

They were gone, all of them. But what had made them go? Something sudden and disastrous, he was sure. Was it sickness—a pestilence of some kind? Smallpox perhaps—or cholera! He shivered and was starting hastily toward the door when his boot struck something that rattled and spun away across the split log flooring.

He went closer, stooping down to see what it was. The flickering beam of the candle shone on bright steel, and he discovered that the thing he had kicked was a butcher-knife, heavy and sharp. For two or three inches above the point it was stained with the brownish red of dried blood.

Bill stared at the knife, a horror-stricken thought forming in his mind. If it was murder that had been done here, he might even now be in the same

room with a dead man. His first impulse was to run
from the bunk-house, but he steadied himself, waiting till his knees stopped trembling. Whatever had
happened it was his duty to find out. Setting his
teeth and shielding the candle flame from the draft
he went slowly around the room, peering into
every bunk, throwing the light into every corner.
The thing he dreaded to find was not there. Except
for the evidence of the knife the inhabitants of the
place might simply have gone out for an evening
stroll.

But the boy knew it was not as simple as that.
Firing a kiln of bricks was no job to abandon without good reason. He blew out the candle and picked
his way back through the dark yard to the spot
where he had left his pack. And just as he reached
the shelter of the lean-to, it began to rain.

.   .   .   .

For a full minute Bill stood under the dripping
roof, looking out and trying to decide what he
should do next. He wanted to leave this place. But
the rain was falling harder all the time. There were
no breaks in the dense darkness overhead. Instead
of another shower he knew he was in for an all-

night downpour, and here under the kiln-roof he could at least keep warm and dry.

He went to the woodpile and dragged cordwood sticks over to the fire-holes in the wall of bricks. One at a time he thrust them end-first through the openings. The dry birch and oak caught fire with a crackle as it fell on the bed of hot coals. By the time he had stoked the last of the little furnaces, fresh flames were roaring cheerfully inside the kiln.

Bill took the little stew-pan from his duffel-pack and set it under the eaves to catch rain-water. Then he sat down with his back against the tin trunk and munched the remnants of his bread and cheese.

It was a gloomy meal. When he had finished and stretched himself on his oilskin beside the deserted kiln he had nothing to do but think. First he attempted to erase from his mind the grim picture of the knife in the bunk-house. After all, it was just a butcher-knife. Maybe it had been used to cut up fresh meat for the stew. But those bloodstains on the blade? They were not along the edge, he remembered, but clustered thick and dark at the point.

Brick-makers were queer, outlandish people, he knew. Irishmen from the bogs, many of them, willing to live like animals and work long hours for the small wages they could earn. He had seen them, stripped to the waist and gray with clay, running between the striking-mold and the dry-yard with their boards of wet new bricks. He tried to imagine what might have happened that afternoon. A drinking bout followed by a fight, perhaps. But why had they all run away afterward?

The warmth from the ovens made him drowsy and he found the puzzle too much for his weary brain. Once more before he went to bed he made the rounds of the fires, throwing on wood. Then he lay down on the hard clay floor and let his tired muscles relax. In a few minutes the drum of rain on the roof had lulled him to sleep.

He woke twice in the night and roused himself each time to feed the kiln with wood. The next time his eyes opened it was to the glitter of early sunlight on wet clay and timber. For a moment he lay in a daze unable to account for his strange surroundings. Then he scrambled up, cramped and stiff, threshing his arms to get the circulation started.

There would be no breakfast, he remembered hungrily. At least there would be none unless he went to the bunk-house and helped himself to provisions, and his stomach revolted at that idea. He would go on, he decided, till he found some farmhouse or tavern where he could get a bite.

Bill wrapped his belongings, arranged his pack, and was ready to sling it over his shoulders when he remembered the kiln. As long as he had kept the fires going all night he thought he might as well throw on more wood before he left. So he made the circuit of the structure once more, stoking each red oven-mouth.

He was just carrying the last armful of sticks from the woodpile when a thud of horses' hoofs came to him out of the alder scrub. In another moment two mounted men rode into the brickyard clearing.

One of them was big and fair-haired and portly. He wore a fine blue coat and rode a solidly built black horse. His companion was a thin, lantern-jawed, scowling man, hunched in the saddle. Across the withers of his rawboned bay he held a grim-looking shotgun, and a metal badge gleamed in the lapel of his old jacket.

They were halfway across the open space when they caught sight of Bill and reined in, staring.

"Who are you?" growled the man with the gun.

Before Bill could answer the other spurred his horse and rode nearer. "Easy, Dan'l," he called. "It's only a lad—no likeness to the one we're after."

He swung down from the saddle and walked toward the boy, leading his horse. "No need to be scared, sonny," he said briskly. "You're a peddler, I judge. Just stop by here this morning?"

Bill shook his head. "I came in before dark last night, looking for shelter," he answered. "The rain caught me, so I slept here by the kiln."

"You did!" The big man sounded surprised. "And you didn't see anybody—or hear any commotion?"

"No," said Bill. "I went to the bunk-house but there was nobody there. Looked like there'd been a rumpus of some kind."

"So there was," the man nodded, still staring at him. "Son, you're luckier than you know. The cook went crazy yesterday afternoon. When the men came in to supper he was waiting for 'em with a butcher-knife. Cut two of 'em pretty bad before they could get out, and as far as we know he's still hanging 'round here."

Bill's cheeks went pale. "G-golly!" he choked. "A crazy man! Guess I *am* lucky!"

The big man stooped and glanced into the nearest fire-door. Then he looked at Bill again curiously.

"I own this yard," he said. "You've been putting more wood on, haven't you?"

"Yes," the boy told him. "Hope you don't mind. I figured maybe the fires ought to be kept up, even if everybody seemed to have left."

"Know anything about brick?"

"Not much—but I've been around brickyards before."

"Well, it's a good thing for that kiln that you kept it going. Here—I owe you some wages." The man's hand came out of his pocket and the next instant Bill was staring incredulously at a crisp two-dollar note that had been placed in his palm.

He tried to stammer some sort of thanks, but

the owner of the brickyard was already mounting his horse. He waved to the boy, rejoined his companion, and the pair cantered off in the direction of the bunk-house.

Bill squatted on his haunches to work his arms through the pack-straps. As he straightened up he saw a four-foot length of hickory sapling, nearly the thickness of his wrist, that had fallen from the cordwood pile. If there was a madman loose in the countryside it might be a comfort to have such a staff in his hand. He picked it up, "hefted" it, and felt the smooth gray bark against his palm. Thus armed he went boldly along the path that led through the thicket and in a few minutes he was out on the highway again.

It was a fine morning. He had money in his pocket—as much as he could have earned in a full week at the mill—and though he was hungry, that was a matter that could soon be remedied. He whistled gaily as he went down the hill.

In the valley before him was a cluster of trim, white-painted houses with a church spire rising from among bare trees. A quarter of an hour of brisk walking brought him into the village street,

28

and he sniffed the air eagerly as he caught the smell of breakfasts cooking.

The inn was easy to find. Its freshly painted sign hung from a post at the edge of the road—a scowling eagle with wings spread against a vivid background of blue. Sounds of bustling activity came from the tavern yard. The eastbound stage had stopped for breakfast and a change of horses, and the stable-boys were leading out the fresh teams as Bill drew near.

A red-faced coachman came out of the taproom wiping his mouth with a bandanna. He carried his whip with an air of some importance and stopped by the wheel-team to peer at the mammoth silver watch he fished from his pocket. "Landlord," he shouted peremptorily, "tell them passengers to swaller their vittles an' git out here. We're leavin' in two minutes, exact."

Bill watched the proceedings with interest. Fairfield was off the main coach-roads and he had seldom seen such a spectacle as this. The hostlers buckled the harness and hooked the trace-chains smartly. One of them held the fidgety leaders' heads while the other passed the reins up to the driver, who had clambered to his box.

"All aboard for Concord!" he bellowed. "Them as ain't out here'll be left behind!"

His warning brought no apparent result, nor did he seem to expect it. He sat there with the reins in his fist and muttered his comments on the inconsiderateness of the traveling public. At last the dining-room door opened and half a dozen chatting passengers strolled out to take their places in the coach. When they were all safely seated, the stable-boy sprang away from the horses' heads, the coachman blew a ringing blast on his horn, and the stage rocked out of the yard at a spanking trot.

Bill drew a long breath and went in to breakfast. When he set down his pack by the door a maid was already clearing away the coach-passengers' plates. Only one other guest was seated at the long table—a weather-browned, big-boned countryman in homespun.

"You can set there," said the maid, indicating a place opposite, and Bill sat down. The stranger eyed him calmly, munching a doughnut the while.

The boy ordered porridge, ham and eggs and coffee. It was an extravagant breakfast that would cost him all of a shilling—twelve and a half cents. But he was feeling both rich and ravenous. He had started eating before his table-companion spoke.

"Travelin' fur?" he asked mildly.

"All the way to Ohio, if my feet hold out," Bill replied.

"That's quite a piece. I'm haulin' through to Brattleboro today, an' I can set ye acrost the river if ye don't mind ridin' a freight-wagon. That tin trunk o' yourn must git sort o' heavy sometimes."

"It does," Bill grinned. "And I don't care how I travel, as long as I cover the miles. How soon do we start?"

CHAPTER

IT still lacked an hour of noon when the big wagon lumbered over the brow of the last hill and started down toward the Connecticut, flowing blue between its high banks. Bill, who had never been beyond the borders of his home state, felt a stirring in his blood as he looked across into

THREE

the hazy folds of the Vermont hills.

The horses—a big pair of long-striding bays—
settled back contentedly into the breeching, while
the teamster pushed down the brake. Hauling a
light load westward, he had ridden at Bill's side all
morning instead of walking by the nigh horse's

flank.

Outside of asking the boy a few questions he had done very little talking. Now the long down-grade to the river seemed to loosen his tongue.

"Thought, when I was your age, I'd sort o' like to go off to far parts myself," he said shyly. "Never got to do it, though—'cept fer haulin' down to Portsmouth an' once to Boston."

He chewed on a dry grass stem and looked off over the Vermont hills. "Reckon you'll foller the Erie Canal," he remarked. "That oughta be somethin' to see. I been told the boats run end to end, pretty nigh, an' every one of 'em carryin' twenty or thirty ton o' freight. One team o' hosses does more work'n ten, haulin' on the road. Good thing fer me we got too many hills 'round here to dig canals. Guess I'd be out of a job."

As they neared the foot of the hill he released the brake and clucked to the horses. "Ferry's comin' in," he explained. "Don't want to wait over a trip."

They rolled down to the landing at a trot and saw the ferry-man about to lift the gang-plank. A buggy, an ox-team and a dozen sheep were already loaded on the long flat-bottomed boat. At the teamster's hail the plank was left down and the horses stepped cautiously aboard. The sheep had to be crowded to both sides to make room for the wagon. There were a few sarcastic remarks from the drover in charge of the flock but he was finally pacified and the ferry started across.

Bill watched the ferry-man and his helper take their places at the fore and aft cranks. A long cable, stretching from one bank of the river to the other, passed around two wheels on the upstream side of the boat. When the cranks, geared to the cable-wheels, were turned, the craft moved slowly forward like a man pulling himself along a rope.

After twenty minutes they creaked in against the landing on the Vermont side. The buggy drove off first, then the sleepy-eyed oxen, then the sheep, bleating with fright, and at last the wagon-team scrambled up the sloping gangway to solid earth.

The pike swung southward along the low-lying ground close to the river. " 'Tain't but three-four mile into Brattleboro from here," the teamster told Bill. "I got a friend lives down the road a piece an' we'll stop there fer dinner."

They baited the horses and ate the plain fare at the farmer's table. Bill offered to pay for his meal but their host wouldn't hear of it. His wife, a plump, pleasant-faced woman, seemed to take a motherly interest in the young peddler and asked to see some of the goods he carried in his pack.

"That lace is real pretty," she said, holding up a piece. "The women-folks out there in the backwoods ought to hanker after such things. Reckon you'll have no trouble sellin' your notions if the prices ain't too high."

"They'd probably seem high to you, living here in the East where things are cheap," Bill explained. "I don't aim to begin selling till I get where there aren't any stores. Goods'll be worth more there."

When the wagon was ready to start, the woman insisted that Bill take a generous package of cold meat and bread and butter. "You're goin' on from Brattleboro, this afternoon," she urged, "an' land knows where night'll find you."

As it turned out, Bill was glad he accepted her gift. He bade farewell to the friendly wagoner when they reached the town, and pushed on up the westward hills at a brisk pace. When sunset came he was in lonely, wooded country, out of sight of any farm.

He chose a bit of high ground, sheltered by bushy young pines, and made his first camp in the

open. With no ax to help him, the job presented some difficulties. However, he collected enough dead branches to throw up a rough lean-to, and dry wood for a fire was not hard to find. With his big knife he scraped tinder out of the heart of a decaying pine log. Brown pine-needles caught the flame when he had touched off the tinder with his

flint and steel. And in a few minutes he had a comfortable blaze going. It was beginning to get dark
in the woods when he went down the hill to see if
he could locate water.

The ground dropped sharply away before him
and he floundered through a thicket toward the
bottom of the ravine, poking a path with his hickory stick. He was making so much noise that he
was almost on top of it before he heard the sound
—a faint, half-human moaning. Bill stood still, his
heart pounding with sudden excitement. Then it
came again, just beyond the brush at his right.
He took a cautious step or two and parted the
branches to peep through.

There was just light enough for him to see a tiny
spring bubbling out of a hollow in the rocks. And
beside it, lying on a patch of moss, was a half-
grown hound puppy. The dog looked up at him
with sorrowful eyes and its tail wagged feebly.

"Gosh!" Bill murmured. "What's the trouble,
little feller?" He knelt quickly by the side of the
black and white puppy and stroked its cringing
head. Then he saw that one hind leg stuck out
awkwardly. On the end of it, gripping the foot

with cruel iron jaws, was a trap. And the chain and clog had become so tangled with the brush that, try as he would, the dog had been unable to reach the water.

It took Bill only a moment to release the tension of the trap and get it off. At once the puppy crawled forward, plunging its muzzle into the spring and lapping the cold water in thirsty gulps. The drink seemed to give it new strength. It scrambled up on three legs and tried to lick Bill's hand.

"You got yourself in a fix, sure enough," the boy grinned. "Feeling better now? Come on with me and I'll give you some supper."

He filled his little kettle with water and made his way back to the camping place, the puppy limping close at his heels.

Bill put more wood on the fire and hung the kettle on a crotched stick over the flames. He had a little packet of tea in his bundle and when the water boiled he made himself a steaming drink to go with the bread and meat. While he was eating he fed generous scraps to the hound, which sat snuggled against his knee.

"Wonder who owns you, pup?" the boy asked.

"And what do they call you? If we're goin' to be camp-mates tonight, seems like I ought to have some name to talk to you by. How about Prince? Don't like that? Well, Rover, then. No, that's too common. I've got it—your name's Jody. There was a young 'un named Jody Smith in school that looked like you. Sort o' pitiful an' meaching. Here, Jody—answer to it an' I'll give you a piece o' meat."

When supper was over Bill pulled enough hemlock tips to make a soft bed under the shelter and fed the fire with an old stump that would burn a long time. Then he stretched himself comfortably before the fire. It was good to have the young hound for company. Bill knew he would have been pretty lonesome there in the woods by himself. He talked to Jody and petted him for the better part of an hour before they curled up together on the bough bed.

The night was clear and still. Overhead, through a cranny in the loosely piled branches of the lean-to, Bill could see a single star. There were faint rustlings and scratchings close by in the woods, where small creatures went about their nightly business, and once an owl hooted dolefully before it swooped by with a whisper of wings. Jody lifted his head and listened, then snuggled down again beside his new friend. There was something so completely trusting in the young dog's action that Bill reached over and gave him a comradely pat. It was a lucky chance, he thought, that had brought them together. He was smiling as he dozed off to sleep.

CHAPTER

AT the first peep of day the little hound jumped up, shook himself and pushed a cold nose into Bill's neck. It was an effective awakening. In five minutes they were on the road with the sunrise behind them.

The boy had half expected that Jody and he

FOUR

would part company at the next farm. It seemed
likely that the puppy had strayed from some house
in the neighborhood and would be only too glad to
find his way home. But they tramped a long distance before a break appeared in the woods. The
first dwelling they saw was two or three miles

from their camping-place.

Bill turned in on the path that led to a small, neat farmhouse. The boy who answered his knock at the kitchen door was about his own age, tousle-headed and scowling. "We ain't buyin' nothin' from peddlers," he snapped.

"That's not what I came for," Bill replied quickly. "One thing I wanted was to ask if this was your dog. I found him caught in a trap back in the woods."

There was no recognition in the other lad's face but he looked a little more friendly. "Ain't a bad-lookin' little dog," he commented. "No—he don't belong to us, an' I never seen him at any o' the neighbors'."

"Well," Bill grinned, "I guess I'm glad to hear that. We've taken sort of a shine to each other—haven't we, Jody?"

At the mention of his name the young dog bounded up to lick his hand. "The other thing," Bill went on, "was to see if we could buy some breakfast—"

Before he could say any more a woman appeared in the doorway back of the boy. "What's this?" she asked briskly. "Somebody hungry out here? Don't talk about buyin' breakfast at my house, sonny. Land's sakes! We got plenty to eat, such as 'tis, an' you're welcome. Lay off yer pack an' come right in."

The meal she gave Bill was a good one, and he finally persuaded her to take a few cents for a lunch of cold food which she put up for him. Before he left, the son of the house had thawed out so far as to bid him a friendly good-by and wish him luck on his journey. As he took the road again he had a warm and pleasant feeling toward the world. If all the people he encountered were as hospitable as these Vermonters he would fare well indeed.

Jody's injured foot looked much better that morning. He trotted at Bill's side with only an occasional limp, and the way seemed shorter because the boy had a companion to talk to. They must have covered a dozen miles up and down the hills before they stopped for their noon meal.

Bill had finished eating and was sitting on a ledge of rock, looking up at the ridge he had to climb, when a sound of music came from the valley below. It was too faint for him to catch the air but there was a strange, exciting lilt to it, like the music of fairy fiddles. Jody had heard it long before his master. He stood with his long flop ears cocked down the road and as the sound came louder he tilted back his head in a quavering howl.

"Hush, boy!" Bill told him. "Listen!"

The tune was clearer now. Bill recognized it as "Turkey in the Straw," played over and over on some instrument that was strange to him. It stopped at length and they could hear the thud and clink of many hoofs, out of sight beyond a turn in the road. Then a man's voice rang out clearly. "Hup! Get on, Joe! Come up, Martha!" And they caught the sharp hiss and crack of a whip.

At that instant the cavalcade came into view. A quick-stepping team of blacks was pulling a buckboard, to the tail of which were tied the lead-ropes of half a dozen other horses. A tall, thin, dark-visaged man lolled on the seat with one leg dangling over the side. And in his hands he held a queer-looking, bellows-like contrivance, gaudily painted and decorated with mother-of-pearl.

When he was abreast of the boy and the dog he stopped his team with a loud "Whoa!" and sat there looking at Bill. His features were sharp, like those of a fox, and there was a look of ironic amusement in his roving black eyes. His dress was curious, too. Though there was mud on his boots, his long, indolent legs were encased in tight-fitting doeskin pantaloons and he wore a dandified bottle-green tail-coat with brass buttons. His hat, tilted back on his head, was broad-brimmed and weather-beaten.

"How now, my lad?" he called, with a grin that showed a mouthful of white teeth. "Sitting at ease when there's a hill to climb? For shame! You should be up and doing!"

Bill returned his stare without answering and the man laughed. "Come on," he said, moving over on the seat. "Plenty o' room here and I can see the pack's a heavy load. So up with you."

Bill hesitated. There was something about this fellow he did not like, but the hill was both steep and high. He swung the tin trunk onto the buck-board, setting it beside a pile of bags that looked as if they held grain. Then he climbed aboard and took his place beside the driver. "Thanks," he said. "I'll be glad of a lift. I guess my dog'll follow all right. Come on, Jody."

As the team started forward again the little hound trotted obediently alongside, keeping a wary eye on the clopping feet of the led horses.

The oddly dressed stranger gave Bill a quizzical glance. "It takes no great power of perception," he said, "to place you as an itinerant vender of notions—in brief, a peddler. And your name?"

Bill was irritated by the man's pedantic talk, but he had accepted the ride and might as well be polite. "Bill Crawford," he said, "of Fairfield, New Hampshire. I take it you're a horse-trader?"

The man flashed those white teeth again. "You are addressing Alonzo Peel," he replied. "A name commonly shortened to 'Lonzo' or plain 'Lon' by my extensive acquaintance. I am—ahem—a purveyor of man's noblest and most abused friend, the horse. It is my privilege to rescue such poor beasts as these"—he waved a hand toward the troop in the rear—"from men who mistreat them, and to find them new homes and more amiable masters."

A pretty fancy way to put it, Bill thought, but

he made no comment. All the way up the hill Mr. Peel continued to roll resounding periods off his ready tongue. As they neared the summit of the ridge he pointed with his whip to the right.

"Yonder majestic peak," he told the boy, "is known in the rustic phrase of the untutored natives as Hogback Mountain. What a name!"

After a few moments of silence the horse-trader wrapped the reins around the whipstock and picked up the curious gadget Bill had first seen in his hands. He put his palms through leather loops on the sides and fingered a double row of white buttons. As he pulled the bellows open a wailing chord of music issued from it, so sudden and loud that the boy gave a start.

Peel laughed. "No cause for alarm, my young friend," he said. "Doubtless you heard my music before I overtook you. This"—he released another flood of sound—"is a newly invented instrument called an accordion. I got it from an Italian who was—er—temporarily in want of funds. It whiles away many lonely hours on the highway."

He played the thing with real skill, Bill had to admit. Deftly now he swung into a tune that the boy recognized as "Buffalo Gals." The jigging notes echoed among the pines and the horses, trotting downhill now, pricked up their ears and snorted.

For an hour the man kept on playing, giving no apparent attention to his passenger except an occasional side glance from his shifty black eyes. Bill, on his part, decided he preferred the trader's music to his talk. He had time to look around at the Green Mountain country and at the horses trailing behind the buckboard. They made a strangely assorted group, he thought. A very old, bony, stringhalty gray hobbled beside a sturdy Canada "chunk," powdered with dust but in prime condition. There were a pair of strong young roan drafters and a fidgety-acting brown saddle-horse with slim legs and a fine head. And jogging drowsily on the outer fringe of the procession was an ancient, fat little mare, her rusty chestnut coat shaggy with winter hair. Bill wondered if she had Morgan blood. In spite of her clumsy gait and homely appearance there was a Morgan look about her nodding head.

After a while Alonzo Peel laid down his accordion and shot a searching glance at the boy beside him. When he spoke he had dropped his high-flown language. "It'll be a long walk to Ohio," he said. "May take you a month to get there. Why do you go afoot?"

Bill looked at him in puzzlement. "How else would I go?" he asked.

The trader flashed his fox-like grin. "Horseback, of course," he replied. "I've got all kinds and all prices in my string. That old gray for instance. He's a bit out o' flesh, perhaps, but he'd carry that trunk o' yours on a long journey."

"Looks like he might go on a long journey any minute," Bill grunted. "No, I reckon he wouldn't be much help."

"You're missin' a bargain," the trader smiled persuasively. "I got him cheap in a trade, and I'd let him go for eleven dollars."

"Makes no difference," Bill told him. "I haven't any money—not that much anyhow—even if I wanted him."

"Ah—no money," the man nodded. "But maybe you've got some trinkets in your pack that I'd find useful. I suppose you're carryin' seventy-five or a hundred dollars' worth o' goods. Just a small part o' that would fix you up with a genuwine ridin' animal."

"I'd rather keep my stock till I can sell it for cash," Bill replied patiently. "If I was aiming to buy a broken-down horse—which I'm not—I wouldn't want the gray anyhow. I'd be more interested in the old mare."

"Martha?" Peel grinned. "Oh, no—not her, my lad. She's not for sale. And I won't tell you why, because then you'd know as much as I do."

He winked slyly and slapped the reins on the horses' rumps. "You travel with me a spell and we might make a trade yet," he added with a chuckle.

Bill thought otherwise but he kept his opinion to himself. He was beginning to regret having accepted a ride with this unaccountable horse-dealer. They were trotting on a down-grade now. The boy looked around for Jody and saw him far behind, trying to keep up on three legs.

"Mister," he said. "I'm afraid you'll have to stop and let me get my dog. His foot's hurt an' he can't go this fast."

"Sure—sure," Peel agreed affably. "Take him

aboard. He won't weigh us down much."

The horses were slowed to a walk and Bill went back after Jody. He lifted the panting puppy and started toward the buckboard, talking to the little dog and stroking his head. Suddenly he heard a sound that made him look up. It was the crack of a whip. The horses had plunged into a gallop and the whole cavalcade was going away in a cloud of dust.

For a second Bill was speechless. Then his temper flared. The low-down robber—trying to steal his trunk! "Hey!" he yelled. "Stop, you!"

He dropped the dog and ran after the trader with the speed of desperation. For a few strides he seemed to hold his own, but the careening buckboard was picking up momentum with every turn of the wheels. Then something happened. Bill saw the led horses floundering in confusion. The dust eddied and cleared and he realized that the vehicle was pulling to a stop. On the ground the old gray nag lay struggling, its neck stretched pitifully by the halter, while the rest of the troop reared and snorted in an effort to avoid trampling their comrade.

The boy kept on running till he reached the

buckboard, red-faced and breathless. Alonzo Peel had climbed down and was untying the rope that held the prostrate gray. Released from its strangling pull the old horse wheezed painfully and lay resting.

"He ain't hurt," snapped the trader. "Just scraped a little. Come on you—get up!"

He aimed a brutal kick at the poor beast's ribs and the gray reared up on shaky knees. Another kick, another struggle, and it got somehow to its feet.

Bill reached up to pull his trunk off the buckboard. He had had enough of the man's company.

"Hey—hold on, sonny," Peel urged. "You're not goin' off mad, I hope. I meant to explain—somethin' scared those pesky nags an' they started to bolt. I pulled 'em in quick as I could, but old Bony here got his feet tangled up."

His smile was disarming, but he had come very close to Bill's side and there was something menacing in the way he rocked on the balls of his feet.

"You just hop up on the seat there with your pup," he advised softly. "We'll make camp in a good place I know, along the road a piece."

The boy hesitated. Peel's version of what had happened was far from convincing but it left him in doubt. Short of calling the horse-trader a liar and a thief he had no valid excuse for breaking away. It was the whimper of the little hound at his feet that made him decide. Jody couldn't walk much farther. He picked the dog up and climbed over the wheel, but as they resumed their journey once more he resolved to be on his guard against any more of Peel's tricks.

Before sundown the trader swung the team into a narrow wood road that branched off to the left along the bank of a stream.

"In my wanderings," he told Bill airily, "I long since came upon this sylvan retreat. It has the advantage of privacy and it offers rest and refreshment for man and beast."

Bill had grown used to the man's sudden changes from everyday talk to this fancy lingo of his. Somewhere in his checkered past, Peel had told him earlier in the day, he had spent a couple of terms at Yale College. Maybe that was where he had picked up those big words.

The boy had something else to think about now.

As the track through the woods wound on and on, seemingly without end, he began to feel uneasy.

"How far is it to Bennington?" he asked. "I should think we could have got there to spend the night."

"Bennington," the horse-trader replied, "is not on my present itinerary. I had—ahem—a slight unpleasantness there, a year or two back. But you'll reach it quick enough in the morning. Just a few miles over the hills."

They came at last to a clearing in the woods. There were gnarled old apple trees and a tangled mat of dead grass, and on the lower side, near the brook, a dilapidated little house. The clapboards were gray and twisted, there were holes in the roof and the door had fallen in. Peel drove up in front of the abandoned dwelling with a flourish.

" 'Light down, passenger," he chuckled. "This is our tavern for the night. I'll let the horses loose to feed in the wild hay here, and we'll have supper goin' in no time. You might fetch some o' them old apple limbs, an' any dry stuff you can find in the edge o' the woods."

With Jody following at his heels Bill brought an

armful of broken branches from under the trees, then set off for the fringe of pines a hundred yards away. It took him a few minutes to collect enough sticks for a fire. When he returned the trader was out of sight in the house, clattering among the pots and pans by the fireplace. Bill passed the buckboard and stopped suddenly with a sinking of the heart. His precious pack was not as he had left it. The straps were pushed aside, and the end of a bit of lace protruded from under the edge of the lid. He had a feeling that the trunk had been opened, pawed through and hastily closed again.

CHAPTER

BILL carried his wood into the house and dumped it on the hearth. He said nothing to Peel about the trunk but proceeded to whittle a pile of shavings and start the fire. The horse-dealer was in a cheerful and talkative mood. He opened the door of an old cupboard and

58

FIVE

brought out corn meal, salt, a flitch of bacon and a tin cannister of tea.

"I pass this way every few months," he told Bill by way of explanation. "There's provisions on the wagon o' course, but I always keep somethin' put by here for emergencies."

The fire was blazing brightly now, and Peel looked around for a kettle. "Here, lad," he said, "we'll need water if I'm to make tea and johnny-cake. Take this down to the brook and fill it."

Bill looked at him speculatively. It was only a few steps to the stream and he could hurry. He didn't trust the horse-trader any farther than he could see him, but this errand seemed simple enough. He picked up the kettle and went down the slope back of the house at a run. In a moment he was back, slopping the water on the doorstep in his haste.

Peel's foxy eyes gave him a quick side-glance. "Gettin' mighty spry, aren't you?" he grinned. He was slicing bacon into the skillet with a long, wicked-looking, sharp-pointed knife. It was no kitchen knife and Bill had not noticed it before. The trader must have had it concealed somewhere under his coat. As he finished the bacon he made a sudden motion, and quicker than Bill's eye could follow, the knife flicked through the air. Staring, the boy saw the point buried two inches deep in the wooden timber that capped the fireplace.

"I've always been real handy with edge tools,"

60

Peel chuckled softly. "Knife-fightin' is a good thing to know, sometimes."

Bill shivered as he set the kettle down on the hearth. If the demonstration was intended as a warning it had produced its effect. The boy found he had little appetite for supper. In fact he was too busy with his thoughts to know what he was eating. Absent-mindedly he fed a few handfuls of corn bread to the dog and went out to look around the clearing.

It was nearly dark now. The horses browsed contentedly in the dry grass and he could hear the steady champing of their jaws. Down by the water a chorus of young frogs peeped shrilly. The idea that had been stirring in Bill's mind began to take definite outlines. He was sure now that Peel wanted what was in his pack—that he was being held virtually a prisoner until such time as the trader was ready for action. There was just one thing to do, and that was get away—now—tonight.

When he returned to the door Peel had stretched himself in front of the fire. Leaning on one elbow he was cutting slivers off a dark twist of tobacco and preparing to fill his pipe. The accordion was beside him on the floor.

"Here," he told the boy gruffly, "take this stuff down to the brook an' wash it good." He pointed to the dirty utensils. "I'll play you a tune 'fore we go to bed," he added, as if to take the sting out of his command.

Bill made no reply. He came slowly over to the hearth and picked up the skillet, tin cups and spoons. When he was outside he moved off noisily in the direction of the brook.

Twenty paces from the house he stopped, laid the things down silently and started tiptoeing back. At the corner of the house he paused, listening. In the stillness above his own heartbeats he could hear the horse-dealer pulling on his pipe. The boy slipped past the door to the dim bulk of the buckboard, lifted his pack in his arms and went quietly back around the other end of the building. Inside, he could hear Peel squeezing a tentative note or two out of the accordion.

"Come on, Jody," Bill whispered, and with the hound trotting behind him he headed for the woods. Once he was past the first small pines he stopped to sling the trunk on his shoulders. Then he stumbled on again, groping his way among the trees in the darkness. In the few seconds he had had for planning his escape he had seen the futility of going back to the road. As soon as Peel missed him he would be sure to follow that way—on horseback if he chose.

Bill was out of hearing from the cabin now, and he made all the haste he could, stumbling forward at a run, careless of brush and briars. At the end of half a mile he pulled up, panting, his boots squelching in water. He must have come to a swampy place at the edge of the brook.

His plan, if it could be called a plan, was to cross to the other side of the stream and spend the night somewhere deep in the woods. In the morning he figured he could cut across to the highway a few miles to the west and resume his journey.

As he stepped forward into the deepening water he wished he had brought along his hickory staff. It was a scary business, wading through an unfamiliar river, when you could neither see nor feel what lay ahead. He shivered as the cold water crept up to his knees. Jody whimpered somewhere behind him and he turned and picked the little dog up. How deep would it get, he wondered? There was no way to find out except to keep going. He gritted his teeth and waded on, and in a moment he was out on the other side, scrambling up a brushy bank.

Bill plowed through the woods for what seemed a long time. His only pause was to empty the water out of his boots. After that he kept moving forward, hoping his sense of direction would not betray him in the darkness.

At last he felt safe from pursuit. He had reached a high knoll carpeted deep with pine-needles, and there he flung himself down, too tired to move. The puppy licked his face and cuddled beside him.

Bill stirred himself after a while. His feet and legs were cold from their wetting and he knew he needed a fire. On the high ground it might be seen. He scrambled down the far side of the knoll and gathered a pile of dry limbs and needles. After a few false starts he got a blaze going in the angle of a ledge of rock. Too tired to make himself a bed, he stretched out with his feet toward the flames and went to sleep.

．　．　．　．　．　．　．

It was morning when he woke, chilled through, his muscles stiff and aching. Jody had been scouting in the woods and now returned to his master, his tail wagging hopefully.

"No breakfast today, little feller," Bill told him, "unless you want to catch yourself a rabbit or something."

The boy pulled his belt a notch tighter and looked at the sky through the tree-tops. It was cloudy and overcast. No sunrise to give him his bearings. He went back to the top of the knoll, pulled off his boots and started to climb a tall pine. It was a hard job for he had to shinny up the first forty feet. After that there were stubs of branches to give him a toe-hold and he made better progress. Eighty or ninety feet from the ground he looked around him.

There seemed to be no break in the forest—no sign of road or clearing. A mile or two away to his right the land looked lower and he thought that might mark the course of the stream he had crossed. In the other direction a range of hills loomed up. He remembered Peel's saying something about hills to cross on the way to Bennington. That would mean they lay to the west. If he bore northward he ought to reach the road in the course of an hour or two.

Actually it turned out to be much longer than that. The country was rugged, filled with rocky ravines and brush-covered slopes that made it impossible to hold a straight course. He plugged along doggedly all through the morning, trying to check his direction by trees and other landmarks. To add to his difficulties it began to rain soon after he started, and it was a bedraggled and weary youngster who came out on the turnpike some time around noon.

All the way through the woods Bill had been turning the adventure with Peel over in his mind. In a way he was ashamed of having run away. Among boys his own age he had never backed out of a fight and he knew he was nearly as big as the horse-trader. As he sat now, resting by the roadside in the rain, he was almost hoping Peel would make his appearance. Then he remembered the whizz and glint of the thrown knife and got a cold feeling in his stomach. No, he wasn't ready to tangle with the fox-faced man—not yet.

Before starting on, he carried the trunk to a

comparatively dry spot under a bushy jack-pine and examined its contents. As nearly as he could tell his trade goods were all there. Probably the horse-dealer had merely been trying to see if he had anything valuable. He straightened out the ribbons and laces, closed the cover again and got into his pack-harness.

The rain stopped when he had been tramping westward for half an hour. With the sun shining, he was able to forget the empty ache in his belly. Surely he would come to a farmhouse soon where he could get something to eat. He was nearing the foot of the mountain ridge now, and there before him, just where the road started to climb, he saw a white house and a snug set of buildings among cleared fields.

Bill hurried forward, spurred by his hunger. He was about to turn into the yard when an elderly man with spectacles and gray chin-whiskers came out of the door. He was carrying a worn leather bag and looked like a doctor. He walked quickly toward a white horse, harnessed to a two-wheeled chaise, that stood by the hitching-post.

When he caught sight of Bill he stopped. "Don't

believe they want to buy anything today, young man," he advised briskly. "Sick folks in there."

"Oh," said Bill, disappointed. "I was figuring I might get dinner, but in that case I won't bother 'em."

The doctor eyed him keenly, from his muddy boots to his wet and battered hat. "Get in the shay," he said. "Yes, your dog, too. Haven't had dinner myself yet, but we won't be long. Got a hoss here that won't admit there's any such thing as hills—when he's headed home, that is."

Tied to the post, the white horse had had a sleepy look. But once on the road and pointed westward, he proceeded to make good on the doctor's boast. Bill had never seen such a puller, and said so. They were on the steepest part of the climb before the animal dropped his eager trot to a walk.

"Yessir," the doctor chuckled. "He's the kind of a hoss I need in my business. When I've been out all night on a case, all I have to do is get in the shay an' go to sleep. He's got such a nose for oats he puts out straight for home. When I wake up we're in the barn."

He laughed again and pushed back his worn

beaver hat. "Year or so back," he said, "a hoss-trader come through Bennington an' tried to buy him. 'Course I wouldn't sell, but that night Whitey disappeared out o' the barn. The hoss-trader was gone too. Looked mighty bad. But shucks! You know what happened? Two days later I heard a hoss whickerin' out in the yard, an' there was Whitey, with a busted halter round his neck! Just got hungry an' decided to come home."

"Gosh!" Bill breathed. "Did they ever catch the thief?"

The doctor shook his head. "Nobody had any proof it was the trader," he replied. "He's never been back, though."

Bill was busy putting two and two together. "I guess there's crooked horse-traders everywhere," he said. "I wonder—did you know the man's name?"

The doctor scratched his head. "Yeah," he frowned. "I'll see if I can't recall it. He was a queer duck. Wore outlandish clothes an' had the gift o' gab. Hmm—now what was that feller's name? Hold on! I pretty near had it, then. Somethin' about an apple, seems as if 'twas. Peel—'Lonzo Peel—that's what he called himself!"

CHAPTER

FOR a moment or two Bill kept silence. He didn't want to blurt out the whole story of his recent adventure. As he looked back on it he had not cut a very heroic figure. When he spoke at last it was in as casual a tone as he could command.

SIX

"I b'lieve I ran across that feller Peel yesterday," he remarked. "Back near Brattleboro. A tall man, dark, with a face sort of like a fox. He was driving a good pair o' blacks to a buckboard an' had a bunch of other nags tied on behind."

"Sounds like him," the doctor nodded. "Headed

this way?"

"I don't think so. I rode with him a ways, an' he said something about not getting any closer to Bennington than he could help. He'd had a slight unpleasantness there, he said."

The doctor chuckled. "I recollect that's the way the feller talked," he said. "Slight unpleasantness, huh? He'd find it mighty unpleasant if the Bennington Hoss-thief Detectin' an' Pursuin' Association got wind of his bein' in the neighborhood!"

They came into the town at a rattling pace and turned into the driveway of a comfortable white house. The horse never slowed down till he was over the threshold of the barn.

The doctor's wife, a plump, capable-looking little woman, seemed to find nothing strange in his bringing a tattered young peddler in to dinner. She fed them both well and provided Jody with a plate of scraps at the kitchen door.

When Bill had put on his pack and was ready for the road again he tried to tell the kindly couple how grateful he was.

"Don't give it a thought," the doctor grinned. "I like young folks—'specially when they show gumption. You'll be over in 'York State by night —clean out o' New England. See to it when you get on west that nobody thinks any the worse o' Yankee traders 'cause o' you. A reputation for honest dealin' is one o' the best things a man can have."

Though it was nearly mid-afternoon when Bill left Bennington, he traveled at a good pace and covered more than a dozen miles before evening. The weather held fair, and Jody seemed better for his rest in the chaise. His foot, when the boy examined it, was healing properly. He trotted along gaily with hardly a sign of a limp.

Bill had crossed another range of hills and was descending a long slope through a pretty farming country when sunset came. He thought he must have left Vermont, for the houses and barns had a different look. He stopped at one of these places about six o'clock and asked for a meal and lodging.

The housewife had a round, placid face and straw-colored hair. She answered him in a queer dialect which he decided must be Dutch. Yes, she told him, he could have supper for a shilling, and he could sleep in the barn if his dog did not bark.

The food was good, though a little strange to his Yankee palate. He washed at the pump in the barnyard, helped the farmer with his milking and made himself a bed in the half-empty hay-mow.

Next morning he volunteered to clean out the cow-stable and for this the Dutchman gave him breakfast free. You didn't get something for nothing in this part of the world, Bill had discovered.

His journey across Rensselaer County was tranquil enough. He didn't mind doing chores for his meals, and so he made his little supply of cash hold out till he reached the Hudson. At a few places, distant from any town, he tried his hand at selling, but he found the Dutch women were hard bargainers. Peddling, he thought, would be a discouraging business if he had to depend on customers like these. He sold three or four yards of plain cotton goods and a few bits of lace, but his total profit in three days of travel amounted to less than a dollar.

It was a fine spring morning when he caught his first glimpse of the river through a gap in the low hills. The eleventh of April if his reckoning was right—just six days since he had set out from Fairfield. There was a feather of smoke drifting above the blue water. His pulse quickened for he knew it was a steamboat—the first he had ever seen.

He hurried on, craning his neck for a better view of the wonders that lay ahead of him in that broad valley. Soon he could see the whole busy town of Troy spread out along the river-front. Strings of canal-boats moved slowly in the stream, towed by puffing paddle-wheel steamers.

Bill had had a good breakfast that morning, but by noon-time he was hungry again. He had spent the last hour down by the wharves, staring goggle-eyed at the jaunty boaters and hustling longshore-men. And though he had taken no part in their activity, the air of excitement that prevailed seemed to whet his appetite. He looked around for a place to eat and saw several men going into a waterside tavern.

Bill followed them in and set down his pack by the door. He took an empty place near the end of the long plank table and was presently served a plate of corned beef and cabbage. While he ate he listened to the boisterous talk of the teamsters and boaters around him. Strange, fascinating names

rolled off their tongues. The "Michigan Six-Day"
and the "Cayuga Line"—the fight between Redeye
McGilligan and the Buffalo Bully at Number Four
—the bet won by the skipper of the "Flying-
Machine" Packet when his boat broke the record
from Rome to Lockport.

The boy's excitement grew. This Erie Canal was
something to see, as the Brattleboro wagoner had
told him. In his vague plans he had expected to
cross New York on foot by the Great Western
Turnpike. Three hundred miles of dusty tramping
seemed a dismal prospect now that he knew of a
more romantic way of travel. He wondered how
much the packet-boats charged for deck passengers. Seven or eight dollars from Troy to Buffalo,
he thought. But they traveled day and night and
made the trip in four days. If he could get a job of
some kind and save his money he might have
enough for the fare in a couple of weeks.

By the time he had finished his pie most of the
men had left the tavern and gone back to work.
At the other end of the table a single guest still sat
sucking gloomily at a clay pipe. He was a big,
hulking, tough-looking man with a two-day stub-

ble of dark beard on his cheeks.

"Never see sech a place," he grumbled to the tavern-keeper. "Every Tom, Dick an' Harry 'long the wharves is workin' at good wages. Turn up their noses at what I can pay, or else they think they're too good to work with hosses."

The landlord drew a tankard of beer and set it in front of the disgruntled customer. "I thought Willie Fink was your driver," he remarked. "What become of him?"

"Yah!" The man at the table made a disgusted face. "That poor, dumb foozle-head! He's jest the cause o' my trouble. Went down to Albany night 'fore last to blow his pay an' got wild drunk. There was a fight an' he had to git in it. Time it was over he was on the floor with his arm broke in two places. An' me with a full load o' farm tools ready to move! Don't talk o' Willie Fink to me!"

"I dunno, Buck," said the landlord placatingly. "They tell me it's hard times, but folks don't seem to want to work 'round here, an' that's a fact. Fur's I know you'll jest have to set in the basin a spell. How long 'fore Willie's arm'll be patched up ag'in, do you reckon?"

"Too long!" the big man growled as he drained the tankard and rose lumbering to his feet.

He was about to leave the tavern when Bill got up his courage to speak.

"I take it you need a man," he said. "If it's a job around horses, I guess you'll find I'd be all right—"

"You!" The burly fellow's voice was scornful. "You don't look like no canawler. What boats you been on?"

Bill stared. "Boats?" he asked. "I thought you said it was a driving job."

"Haw, haw!" roared the inn-keeper. "He's a greenie, all right, Buck. But, by gum, you got you a driver!"

The man scowled at Bill from under heavy black brows. "Anybody drives fer me," he said, "has got to do more'n handle hosses. He's got to be able to walk thirty mile a day an' never whimper. He's got to keep the stable clean an' the harness mended. All I don't ask him to do is fight fer his place at the locks. Come to that, I'll tend to the fightin'. Ten dollars a month is reg'lar boys' pay. Want it?"

"Where you headed for?" Bill asked boldly.

"All the way through to Buffalo, this trip. Why

—what's that got to do with it?"

"I'm bound west," the boy replied, "an' I'd like to work my way on the canal. I reckon you could get another driver in Buffalo, to bring you back."

He waited, hardly daring to breathe, while the man called Buck looked him over with cold appraisal. At length he spat in the sawdust on the floor and nodded grudgingly.

"I'll chance it," he said. "Five dollars fer the one-way trip, an' we'll be startin' fust thing in the mornin' so you better sleep aboard. My boat's the *Mohawk Tiger*. You'll find her tied up in the basin —fourth boat from the end. An' if anybody wants to know why you're there, tell 'em you're drivin' fer Buck Hoyle. I'll be back by suppertime."

With that he tossed a coin on the table and left the tavern. The landlord pocketed the money and came over to Bill's side. "I guess you got a lot to learn about boatin'," he leered. "But Buck Hoyle's the boy that'll teach you! He's a rip-roarin' son o' Satan when he gits in a fight. You may see some fur fly, though there ain't many left on the canal that are willin' to tangle with Buck. He'll treat you fair enough if you don't cross him. But watch out when he's in likker!"

Bill paid for his dinner, picked up his pack and called Jody. He was eager to see the canal-boat on which he was to earn his way to Buffalo. A question or two and a walk of half a dozen blocks brought him to the basin. To his landsman's eyes it was a scene of enchantment. Moored end to end along the bulkheads a hundred blunt-nosed craft rocked in the eddies. Some of them were old and weatherbeaten, but the majority gleamed with new paint. Yellows and blues and reds, stripes and fancy scrolls adorned their hulls and cabins.

It was not hard to find the *Mohawk Tiger*. Her lower parts were black, with a broad band of orange around the gunwale, and her stern cabin was painted with the same vivid colors, laid on in alternate stripes. She lay deep in the water. The hold, amidships, took up a good two-thirds of the boat's length, and it was filled now with cargo, lashed down under a big tarpaulin. Forward there was another structure with a broad door opening in its side. At first Bill wondered what this might be, but he guessed when he heard the stamping of a horse. A stable—right on board the boat!

There was a narrow plank reaching from the shore to the afterdeck. After a moment's hesitation Bill crossed over and stood on board, wondering what to do next. Jody did not trust the plank. He made a flying leap to land at his master's side, and it was while the boy was leaning down to pat the puppy's head that the cabin door opened.

"Oh!" said a startled voice. "I thought it was Mr. Hoyle come back."

Bill saw a girl of about his own age standing at the foot of the little flight of steps. She had coal-black hair done up in a red ribbon, and her cheeks were bright with sudden color. For a few awkward seconds neither of them spoke. Bill always felt shy in the presence of girls and this one was alarmingly pretty. He knew that his own face must have grown red.

She was the first to recover. "I suppose you're selling something," she remarked coolly. "Don't believe we need a thing today."

"No—I haven't anything to sell," Bill stammered. "I mean—yes, I'm a peddler, but I'm not trying to sell *you* anything. I'm your new driver."

The girl smiled. "Oh," she said, "that's different.

Mr. Hoyle had about given up hope of finding one. Did he really hire you?"

Bill wasn't exactly sure how she meant that question. "He seemed to be satisfied," he replied stiffly. "I guess I can handle the job. I'm 'most seventeen and used to horses."

"All right," she nodded. "You can put your things forward, in the stable. There's a berth there but I don't know how clean you'll find it."

The interview appeared to be over, but the boy still stood there, shuffling his clumsy boots. "My name's Bill," he told her. "Bill Crawford."

She smiled again, quick and friendly. "Mine's Mary Ann Bennett," she said. "I'm the cook."

With that she disappeared inside and Bill was left staring at the closed cabin door. Mary Ann Bennett. That was a pretty name, he thought. Slowly he took his way forward along the catwalk.

When he opened the stable hatch there was a whinny of greeting from within and he saw the broad sterns of a big pair of red roan horses. Their two stalls fitted neatly into the small space. At one side there was just room for a driver's bunk, and a big grain-box stood against the bulkhead, flanked by a pile of loose hay.

Bill set down his pack and proceeded to make friends with the roans. They sniffed his clothes suspiciously at first but his knowing hands soon won their confidence. Jody kept a prudent distance from their heels and they accepted his company.

The boy's next move was to investigate the place where he was to sleep. It wasn't much of a bed. Just a narrow box between the stall and the bulkhead, filled with matted hay. A pair of foul, dirt-stained blankets lay in a rumpled heap across its foot. Wrinkling his nose, Bill picked them up and carried them to the deck. There was no clothesline but he spread the blankets on the flat stable roof and hoped the April breeze would air them out.

Back inside, he shook up the hay in the bunk, removing the two empty whisky bottles he found there. He was beginning to think he did not care much for Willie Fink.

The rest of the afternoon passed slowly. Bill curried the horses and gave the stable a thorough cleaning. Then, finding no other chores to do, he took a stroll around the basin with Jody. Most of the boats were inhabited, he found. Washes fluttered from the lines and smoke rose comfortably from cabin chimneys. Occasionally a boater, sunning on the afterdeck, nodded a greeting.

When he heard the clink of dishes and smelled suppers cooking he found his way back to the *Tiger*. Buck Hoyle was already aboard. His eyes were bleary and his speech a little blurred but he remembered the driver-boy he had hired.

"Come on down here, young feller," he boomed, as Bill appeared in the companionway. "I took a look in the stable an' you done a good job—yessir —good job." His voice trailed away, then picked up an entirely different train of thought. "All fixed t' start soon's make up a string o' boats to go 'crost—be in the canal in the mornin'."

He waved his huge arm in a sweeping gesture. "Come on, boy—'s time t' eat," he grinned. "How 'bout it, gal—supper ready?"

Mary Ann, standing behind him at the stove, shot Bill a warning look. "Coming right on the table, Mr. Hoyle," she answered cheerfully.

The boy pulled a stool up to the end of the table and in a moment plates of steaming beef stew were set before them. Mary Ann served herself last and sat down opposite Bill. Except for the noises Buck Hoyle made in the process of getting food into his mouth, it was a silent meal. The boater gulped down his coffee before the others had finished. He pushed back his chair and lifted his bulk on swaying legs. "Gotta go see 'bout the towin'," he muttered. "Ol' Andrew Jackson steamboat be 'long pretty soon—goin' take us acrost."

As he lurched toward the stairs Bill started to follow, but a quick hand on his arm stopped him. He looked around at the girl. She waited till the boater had reached the deck before she spoke.

"Keep out of his way," she breathed. "He gets terrible ugly sometimes when he's been drinking."

Bill frowned and looked at the two bunks in the cabin—the big one under the stairs and the one with the blue curtain, across by the stove. "How about you?" he asked. "Aren't you scared to stay here if he's like that?"

The girl lifted her determined chin. "I've got to stay here," she said. "And he's never bothered me. No—I'm not scared. Listen, Bill, I think I hear him going ashore now. You better duck forward and get to bed before he comes back."

CHAPTER

BILL found the bunk in the stable a far more comfortable bed than he had expected. He opened the little square window above it and snuggled down in the hay with Jody beside him. Beyond the planking the horses shifted and stamped, nuzzled in their mangers and

finally lay down with long, puffing sighs. The boy could not get to sleep for a while. He had seen a good many new things that day and the thrill of his prospective journey was still on him. On the other hand, Mary Ann's words had given him something to think about. At first it had seemed almost providential that Buck Hoyle needed a driver, but now he began to have some doubts.

He heard the big boater come on board again, an hour or two later, stumbling and cursing in the dark. Hoyle went forward past the stable, and there was the thump and scrape of heavy cordage on the deck. Then a voice hailed from another boat close by and the slack of a rope splashed in the water. "All fast, there?" the other man asked. Hoyle answered with a grunt and tramped heavily aft again.

Bill raised himself on one elbow, listening. He heard the cabin door open and bang shut again. He wondered what he would do if the black-haired girl screamed. But there was no scream—no sound except the thud of dropped boots and then the peaceful creak that told him Hoyle had tumbled into his bunk. In another moment the boater began to snore gently, and Bill rolled over and went to sleep.

His slumbers must have been sound indeed, for when he woke, the *Mohawk Tiger* was in the canal and it was dawn. Standing up to look out the window he saw a hard-beaten strip of ground that must be the towpath, and above it the gray river-mist rising.

Sounds of activity already came from the boat ahead. When Bill opened the hatch and stepped out he could see the dim shapes of horses on the canal-bank.

"Hey!" a man called. "You, 'board the *Tiger*—stan' by to take yore rope!"

Bill hurried to the bows and hauled in the tow-line, which had been cast off into the water. As he coiled down the last length he heard a step behind him. Mary Ann stood there shivering, holding a shawl around her against the morning chill.

"He's still asleep," she said, with a jerk of her head toward the cabin. "When he wakes up he'll want to be moving. You know how to hitch up?"

Under her direction he dropped the broad gang-plank from the stable hatch to the towpath and put the harness on the horses. When he had led the team ashore, one horse moved up at once into the forward place and the other fell in behind. Mary Ann showed Bill how to fasten the tandem traces and he hooked the towline to the ring in the whif-fletree.

"Guess we're ready to start," he told the girl.

"All right," she said. "I've got the breakfast started so I'll steer for a spell. Soon as the boat's moving along all you have to do is keep the team walking steady."

She went back to the tiller and Bill clucked to the horses. They went ahead cautiously till they felt the rope come taut, then bowed themselves and dug in their toes. Almost imperceptibly at first the boat began to move through the water. As she gathered way the roans stopped their straining and settled into a long, plodding stride. Bill walked behind them, watching the little ripple of water around the *Tiger's* bows—the only visible evidence that she was in motion. It amazed him to see how easily those tons of freight could be hauled on the canal.

They had covered the better part of a mile and the mist had nearly disappeared when he looked ahead and saw another team and another boat coming toward him. In a moment they would meet on the towpath.

"Hey—Mary Ann," he shouted. "What do I do now?"

"Stop the horses," she answered, "and keep out to the right. They'll cross over our slack."

Bill guided the team off the path and halted them, wondering just how the passing would be managed. It was so simple when he saw it that he felt ashamed of himself. Momentum continued to carry the *Tiger* forward and Mary Ann's twist of the tiller took the boat toward the farther side of the canal. The sagging towrope sank to the bottom and the down-coming boat passed over it. As the steersman went by, waving a good morning from his post at the stern, Bill saw that the roans had started up again without any urging. They were old hands at the business and knew the pulling would be easier if the boat wasn't allowed to lose headway.

Bill had been tramping the towpath for an hour when Mary Ann called him to breakfast. "I'll drive," she said, jumping ashore as agilely as any boy. "Mr. Hoyle's up and ready to steer."

The boy handed over the reins and reached the forward deck in a flying leap. Back by the tiller Buck Hoyle slouched on a stool, his unshaven face a mask of ill-humor. He did not even nod a greeting as Bill came aft to the cabin. On the stove the boy found a coffee-pot warming and eggs and bacon sizzling in the pan. He was hungry and the food tasted good. When he had finished he pocketed a few scraps for Jody who was trotting along beside Mary Ann on shore.

He climbed the companion steps and was starting forward when Hoyle's harsh voice stopped him. "Where'd that dog come from?" he asked.

Bill turned and faced him. "He's mine. I thought you saw him with me yesterday."

"Don't let him git within reach o' my boot," the boater growled. "Dogs an' me don't git along." He spat over the side by way of emphasis.

The boy did not say a word. White-faced with anger, he made his way forward again and jumped for the towpath. At the moment he took off, the ribbon of open water between boat and shore suddenly widened, and he found himself floundering waist-deep in the canal, clawing his way up the steep bank. Behind him he heard Hoyle break into a roar of bull-voiced laughter. The boater had deliberately caused his ducking by giving the rudder a well-timed twist.

It was not easy for Bill to keep his temper after a trick like that, but he remembered that trouble with Hoyle now would ruin all his plans for getting to Buffalo. Trying not to show the wrath he felt, he emptied his boots, wrung the water out of his breeches and hurried to catch up with the team.

"That was a pretty mean joke to play on you," Mary Ann murmured as she put the reins in his hand. "You didn't sass him, did you?"

"No," said Bill. "I never opened my mouth, but I guess he could see I was mad. He told me he'd kick Jody if I didn't keep him out of his way."

The girl sighed. "He's generally cantankerous like that in the morning," she said. "You just have to humor him."

She waited for the approaching boat, and Bill could see out of the corner of his eye that Hoyle was steering in close to shore for her.

"That's right," she called to him gaily. "You'd better treat me right if you want any dinner. I've got a pie in the oven!"

.   .   .   .

The day passed slowly for Bill. His boots, still damp from the wetting, began to blister his heels after a few miles of steady walking, and he was glad of the rest he got when they climbed the series of locks below White Horse Rapids.

From a quarter of a mile off he saw them, going up like the steps of a great staircase. Behind him, when they came closer, he heard the long, braying blast of Hoyle's boat horn and a wizened little man came out of the lock-keeper's shack, halfway up the combines. The lower gates were open. Bill, not quite sure what he was supposed to do, kept the horses moving up the ramp till the bow was even with the lower end of the lock. There they stopped of their own accord and the boat drifted neatly in. With a creak of iron the gates shut behind her. Then the upper gates were opened and the *Tiger* rose swiftly on the inrushing water. Before the last eddy had stopped swirling, the lock-keeper motioned Bill ahead. And so they went, lifted from one level to the next with an ease that delighted the boy's sense of Yankee ingenuity.

As they started on again at the top, Mary Ann must have noticed his limping gait, for she said something to Buck Hoyle. Then she called his name. "Hey—Bill! Why don't you ride for a spell?"

"Ride?" he asked.

"Sure—just hop up on the rear horse. This isn't hard pulling, and all the drivers do it when they want a rest."

Gratefully he followed her suggestion. The big roan's back was broad enough to make a comfortable seat, and he rode at ease, surveying the busy canal and the country that spread out on either hand.

At noon, when they tied up for an hour to eat dinner and rest the horses, Mary Ann gave him some mutton tallow to rub on his sore heels. Bill had been careful to shut Jody in the stable when they came on board, but he found that Hoyle's mood had completely changed since morning. Instead of being gruff and quarrelsome, the big boater seemed almost jovial that afternoon.

It was seven o'clock and growing dark when they hauled into Schenectady. Bill, who had walked a good twenty miles since sunup, was ready to turn in as soon as he had fed the team and finished his supper. He sat on the gunwale with his boots off, cooling his feet in the water, and wondered whether he would be able to stand a dozen days of Buck Hoyle without a flare-up. The hulking canalman had dressed in his best clothes and gone ashore as soon as supper was over.

Mary Ann finished washing the dishes and came forward, drying her hands on her skirt. "Seems kind of peaceful with him gone, doesn't it?" she said.

Bill nodded. "I reckon it won't be so peaceful in the morning, though," he answered with a wry grin. "He'll come back drunk again, won't he?"

"Maybe not." She sat down beside him on the gunwale. "He said he was aiming to get a shave and go call on some woman he knows here."

Bill was silent for a moment. In the twilight he could steal a glance at the girl's clear young profile without being observed.

"Look here, Mary Ann," he said at last, "what did you mean when you told me you had to stay here?"

He waited a minute but she did not answer. "Cooking for a tough customer like Hoyle is no life for a—for a nice girl like you," he stumbled on. "What about your folks? Wouldn't they rather have you home?"

She gave him an odd look, friendly and grateful. "I'm glad you think I'm a nice girl," she said quietly. "Most canal cooks aren't. I haven't got any folks except a sister in Ohio. Mother died last winter and I worked for the minister's wife a while. That was in Herkimer. She was a mean woman and used to take out her spite on me, till I ran off a month ago. The only job I could get was with Hoyle. I thought he'd be hauling out to Lake Erie and I could go on to my sister's. But his first trip was only as far as Rome, and then back to Albany. Now we're heading west again, and that's why I mean to stay with him till we get to Buffalo."

"Does he know," Bill asked, "about your plans to leave him there?"

The girl shivered a little. "No," she said. "He thinks he's got a steady cook. He'd pretty near kill me, I guess, if he found out."

Bill stood up and squared his shoulders. "If he should lay a hand on you," he said, with an unexpected tremble in his voice, "I'd—well, I'd stop him somehow."

Mary Ann's laughter rang out, fresh and clear, but she took pity on the boy's embarrassment. "I believe you'd try," she told him soberly. "Don't worry about me, though. I'm used to looking out

for myself. Good night, Bill, and get some rest. We'll be making a long stage of it tomorrow."

Bill was asleep a few seconds after he tumbled into the bunk and he did not even rouse when Hoyle came aboard in the wee hours of the morning. Before daybreak he rolled out to grain and curry the horses. And by the time the sun rose they were on their way once more.

Mary Ann had to steer most of the morning, for Hoyle lay late in bed. They had been moving perhaps an hour when the piercing blast of a horn came from behind them. It was unlike the deep, mellow notes of the freight-boat horns to which Bill had grown accustomed. He looked over his shoulder and saw a four-horse team coming at a trot. At the end of their towrope moved a white and gold boat with a long, windowed cabin amidships.

"It's the Flying-Machine Packet!" Mary Ann called. "And they've got the right of way. Get off the path and give 'em plenty of room."

Hastily, Bill guided the team well to the right and stopped them. Mary Ann swung the *Tiger* out just in time, for the smartly harnessed leaders of the packet team were already spanking past her. The driver rode in a saddle on the nigh rear horse, and cracked his whip merrily for the edification of common folk like Bill.

He stared open-mouthed at the passing boat. The captain and the steersman wore natty blue and gold uniforms, and through the windows of the dining saloon he could see well-dressed ladies and gentlemen at their breakfast. The packet swirled away with another flourish of the horn to warn the next freight-boat ahead, and Bill clucked to the roans.

"That's the way to travel!" Mary Ann sang out. "A hundred and twenty miles in a day and a night! There's a change of horses every couple of hours."

They pushed along most of the morning without stopping. When Buck Hoyle came on deck they were close behind an old gray-painted boat pulled by a pair of brown mules.

"What's the matter up there?" Hoyle bellowed. "Make 'em git over an' let you through, boy!"

The driver of the mule team was a small, seedy, middle-aged man. He looked around uncertainly at the helmsman of the gray boat and tried to hurry the mules with a switch.

"Hey, you!" the big boater roared. "We're comin' through—d'ye hear?" And he rounded out the warning with a string of curses.

The man at the tiller of the other boat was a thick-set, towheaded German. He turned leisurely to survey the bow of the *Tiger*, now only a few yards from his own rudder.

"Aw, go chump in der canawl," he rumbled derisively.

Over his shoulder Bill saw a wicked grin appear on Hoyle's hard face. He was coming forward along the catwalk. "Touch up them hosses," he told the boy. "Run right over the mules if ye want. I'm goin' to find out who 'tis that's jumpin' in the canal."

CHAPTER

THE German dropped the tiller and took a belligerent stance, swinging his hamlike fists. "Chust come over here an' I show you!" he shouted.

As Bill urged the horses forward, the gap between the two boats narrowed swiftly. Hoyle

EIGHT

stepped on the bow post and crouched there like a big cat, waiting. When he jumped it was not directly at his challenger but toward the other side of the tiller-beam, so that he had time to get his balance before the German could reach him.

For a second or two they circled each other,

their booted feet clattering on the deck. Then the blond man made a bull-like rush and Hoyle's shaggy fist swung against his jaw with sledge-hammer force. The German tumbled sidewise, dazed and groping. Before he could even get to his knees the dark-visaged boater seized him by the collar and the slack of his breeches and tossed him over the side.

"Now, you lousy runt," he roared at the driver, "get them blankety-blank mules off the towpath!"

He put the helm over and the gray boat drifted sluggishly out from the bank. The roans quickened their pace. With a surge of water under her bow, the *Tiger* went over the other boat's sagging towline. And blowing, sputtering and shaking his fist, the chastened German scrambled out on the bank behind him.

That was the first fight Bill saw on the canal, but it was by no means the last. The roans pulled a solid thirty miles that second day—past the village of Amsterdam and through to the other side of Fonda. Darkness had fallen before Hoyle finally hailed the young driver and tied up for the night. Bill was staggering with weariness when he came aboard. He ate the food Mary Ann set before him, hardly knowing what it was. And ten minutes later he was asleep in his bunk.

Because he was young and healthy he woke at dawn feeling ready for anything. Buck Hoyle was already on deck when he led the horses out. "Make 'em step, boy," the boater called. "I aim to be up the locks at Little Falls 'fore night."

It was a sunny day, hot except where trees shaded the towpath. Bill left his jacket aboard and tramped along in breeches and shirt with his sleeves rolled up. They stopped only a few minutes for dinner—just long enough to water the sweating horses and give them a bait of grain. Then on to the westward, past Fort Plain and the Mohawk Castle, heading toward a bank of lowering, dark clouds that presaged thunder.

The storm held off all afternoon, but the air was heavy and sultry. When at last they came in sight of the locks it was nearly dark, and a warning rumble echoed in the sky. Buck Hoyle lifted his horn and blew a mighty blast. But as they came closer Bill saw that there were other boats there ahead of them. Their teams stood along the path, browsing the little new leaves from the canal-side willows, and up on the ramp beside the first lock two men stood stripped to the waist. Bill stopped the roans, not knowing what else to do.

At that moment one of the two gladiators by the lock drew back his fist and swung viciously at the other's head. He missed and came lunging in, grappling for the body. Then they were both on the ground in a whirl of thrashing arms and legs. Buck Hoyle had jumped ashore. Now he came past the boy at a heavy-footed gallop, cursing as he ran.

"Here, ye slug-witted gowks!" he bellowed. "Get them tubs out o' the way an' clear the lock or I'll knock both yer heads together!"

He sprang into the struggle, grabbed one of the battling boaters by the waist-band and heaved him ten feet into the bushes. The other staggered up wiping the sweat out of his eyes. He took one look at Hoyle's ferocious bulk and turned meekly down the path. In another moment his erstwhile enemy followed and they both poled their boats away from the bank.

"Come on, boy!" Buck shouted. "Whip up them hosses." And his huge arm beckoned impatiently

106

to Bill. As the *Tiger* slid past into the lock the big boater turned to the crews of the other two craft. "Any pair o' lunkheads wanta fight fer the lock, they're welcome," he advised them. "Only don't do it when Buck Hoyle's in a hurry to go through."

His final words were drowned in a clap of thunder and before the gates had closed behind the boat the rain roared down. Drenched and shivering, Bill guided the team up the ascent and on for another half mile. He was so wet when they finally moored for the night that he had to wring out his breeches, hang them on a harness peg in the stable, and come to supper wrapped in one of the blankets from his bunk. Mary Ann laughed at his appearance at first, but she was quick with sympathy and a cup of hot tea when she realized how chilled he was.

Hoyle was in a good humor that night. Fights, Bill could see, were meat and drink to him, and his chief pride was the reputation he had along the Erie as a rough-and-tumble bruiser.

．　．　．　．　．　．　．

That early thunderstorm seemed to have broken the barriers that held back the spring. The green of grass and of bursting leaves swept up the valley like a tide, flooded past the plodding roans and the boy who trudged at their heels, and drenched the Mohawk country with vivid color. Warblers, making their northward migration, chirped and sang in the groves, and bluebirds and meadowlarks greeted the warm sun with cheerful melody.

Bill felt a lift in his spirits. He went whistling along the towpath, happier than he had been in months. When they hauled through Herkimer he could see crocuses springing in the yards of houses, and even along the canal-bank there were yellow dandelions in the grass. The watery highway was swarming with craft that day, as if the fine weather had brought them out. Boats coming down from the west were constantly passing, and the air was filled with the sound of their horns and the greetings of acquaintances.

The *Tiger* tied up in Utica basin before sunset that evening. When Bill had stabled and fed the horses he washed, slicked up as much as he was able with his limited wardrobe, and went aft to supper.

"I b'lieve I'll take a walk around an' see the town," he told Mary Ann when Hoyle had gone ashore. "You want to come?"

"I'd like to, Bill," she answered, "but I guess I'd better not. Utica isn't so far from home but what there's folks here might know me. I wouldn't want word to get back there that I was a canal cook. Maybe you noticed I stayed below when we came through Herkimer this morning."

He set out alone in the spring dusk, thinking Utica was as fine a city as he had ever seen. Even now, with most of the shops closed for the night, the thronging boaters gave it an air of bustle and importance. Away from the canal and the business district, where elms overhung the quiet streets, he saw fine houses with lawns around them, shining carriages in the driveways, and candle-light in festive windows.

Bill returned through a more squalid part of the town. Down by the basin there were warehouses and taverns crowding close to the muddy street. He could hear boisterous singing coming from the bars where the canalmen had gathered. As he turned a corner he saw a figure ahead of him, outlined for a moment against the yellow light of an open door. It was a man, tall and lean, wearing a

dark tail-coat and tight-fitting, pale-colored pantaloons. At the sound of Bill's step the man looked
quickly over his shoulder, then vanished into an
alleyway. But in that one glimpse the boy had seen
enough to make him beat a hasty retreat. He was
almost sure those sharp, dark features belonged to
his old enemy, Alonzo Peel.

As he hurried away along the dockside, Bill
wondered if the horse-trader had recognized him.
The furtive way the man had disappeared made
him think otherwise. Peel would be much more
likely, Bill thought, to welcome a lonely encounter
with his former prisoner than to hide from him.

Moving quickly and quietly along the dark line
of moored boats, the boy kept looking behind him.
He made certain there was nobody following before he slipped across the gangplank of the *Tiger*
and went forward to the stable. Once inside, with
the hatch closed and fastened, he drew a long
breath of relief.

It was a queer thing, running into Peel like that.
He speculated, as he took off his boots and jacket,
on what the horse-dealer might be doing out here

along the canal. Nothing respectable, he was sure.

"Anyhow, Jody," he told the hound pup with a grin, "there isn't much he could do to us now, even if he did see me."

He stretched himself comfortably in the hay and dropped off to sleep. It was three or four hours later that a low growl from the little dog woke him. Jody was trembling as if he had heard or scented danger. Bill laid a hand on the dog's head to quiet him and sat up to listen. Through the open window he could see starlight and catch the faint sound of water lapping against the boat's side. Then somewhere in the distance along the bank of the basin he heard the soft creak of bootsoles. He got up quickly and looked out the window, but it was too dark to see anything moving in the dim shadows of the warehouses.

After a while the hound turned himself around once or twice and flopped down contentedly in the bunk. Whatever had disturbed him it was gone now, and Bill saw no point in watching longer at the window. But because he had more imagination than Jody, even though his senses were less sharp, he was unable to fall asleep at once. Through his mind the thread of an idea kept running. Was it merely a coincidence, he wondered—this midnight awakening so soon after he had seen the horse-trader?

Those restless hours in the night made Bill over-sleep next morning. He was roused by a pounding on the stable hatch and Mary Ann's urgent voice calling him.

"Get up, Bill!" she said. "It's close to seven o'clock and we should be half an hour on our way before this!"

He tumbled out in haste, pulling on his boots. If Hoyle had been drinking last night they might have a bad morning ahead of them, and he didn't want to give the boater any added excuse for ugliness.

The two boats ahead of them had already pulled out, but astern there seemed to be a commotion of some kind. Bill paused to listen while he was buckling the throat-latch of the lead horse's bridle. A man came running along the basin-side, his boots clumping loud on the beaten turf.

"Hoss-thieves!" the man was shouting hoarsely. "They've stole Ben Egan's team o' blacks! Hoss-thieves!" And he continued to cry the news, his shouts coming fainter and fainter as he ran up the street into the town.

By the time Bill had the team ashore and was fastening on the towline, other men came past talking excitedly.

"What's up?" the boy asked.

"Pair o' hosses stole," one of the crowd replied. "Egan was ashore at the Boater's Fancy most o' the night. His boat's down t'other end o' the basin. Some lowdown skunk took his team right out o' the stable. Big, fine pair o' blacks they was—young hosses, too. We're fixin' to gather up a posse an' go after 'em. Comin', youngster?"

"I got freight to haul," Bill answered. "Get up, you, Prince. Get on, Jerry."

At breakfast, an hour later, Mary Ann was full of conversation about the night's happenings. "Stealing horses is about the worst thing anybody can do, on the canal," she told him. "They'll hang him sure if they catch him. Seems like he couldn't have got very far, and they've sent men out in all directions."

"Maybe he's hiding somewhere right here in Utica," Bill answered thoughtfully. "I didn't tell you—I think maybe I saw him last night."

The girl stared at him, big-eyed with excitement, while he described his earlier adventure with Alonzo Peel. He went on to tell her about the doctor's horse, back in Bennington, and led up to his glimpse of the horse-trader last night by the Utica docks.

"I'll bet he's the man!" Mary Ann nodded emphatically. "But if he's traveling with a string of horses it oughtn't to be long before they come up with him."

All morning the roans held a steady pace, pulling up through Oriskany to Rome. They reached the town a little after dinnertime and tied up for an hour while Mary Ann went ashore to buy supplies. Bill was sitting in the shade beside the team when she came hurrying back. She was breathless with news.

"It *was* Peel," she told him. "They haven't

caught him yet, but everybody in the town was talking about it. And, Bill—there's a reward for him. I saw the paper, nailed up in front of the store. A hundred dollars for the capture of the horse-thief, Alonzo Peel—dead or alive."

CHAPTER

BEYOND Rome the canal made a bend to the southwestward, and Bill tramped along through the afternoon with his hat pulled down to keep the sun out of his eyes. It was a lonesome stretch of country. That night when they tied up, somewhere to the east of Oneida Cas-

NINE

tle, the boy heard the shrill bark of a fox, off in the woods. Jody whimpered restlessly. It took him a long time to settle down, and Bill shared his wakefulness. He lay there thinking about Peel, imagining him and his string of dubiously gotten nags hidden away in some secret clearing like the one he had seen in Vermont. He could picture the horses in his mind's eye—the decrepit gray, the Canada chunk and Martha, the plump old mare with the Morgan look about her head.

For several days they heard no more about the horse-thief chase. Bill, feeling himself an expert driver now, tramped behind the roans as they hauled through Syracuse and the long, watery wilderness of the Montezuma swamps. They passed Weedsport the second day out of Rome, and on the fourth they were hauling up to Rochester.

Bill could hear the thunder of the falls half an hour before the busy town came in sight. The spring torrent of the Genesee, tumbling in its three cataracts toward Lake Ontario, made the towpath tremble under the boy's feet. They crossed the river on the aqueduct and moored at the end of the long flour-mill docks.

After supper Bill was forward in the stable, tending the horses, when he heard voices outside. Two young men in fashionable clothes had stopped opposite the *Tiger's* afterdeck, where Mary Ann was seated by the tiller.

"A pretty piece, by George!" one of the dandies

remarked loudly. "What say, my dear—would you like to see the sights of the town?"

"Come, come!" the other laughed. "I believe the gal has lost her tongue."

Stepping out through the hatch, Bill saw Mary Ann's face flush darkly. She rose and turned her back on her annoyers, and at that moment the cabin door opened. Buck Hoyle was up the companionway in two catlike jumps. He had been shaving in the cabin and was stripped to the waist, the lather still clinging grotesquely to his jowls. Before the pair on the dock had time to retreat he was across the gunwale and striding up to them. Bill saw the silent snarl on his lips and the startled look on the faces of the city men. Then he himself was running toward the group. He wouldn't object to getting in a few blows on his own account.

But there was no fight left in the dandies when Bill reached them. Hoyle's hands shot out, caught each man by the scruff of the neck and smashed their heads together with a hollow thump. Two battered beaver hats rolled in the mud, and the young lotharios sprawled together in a tangled heap.

As they lay there dazed, the big boater uttered the first words he had spoken since he came out of the cabin. "Let that larn ye to keep yer dirty tongues off my gal," he growled. And turning on his heel he went back aboard the boat.

The possessive tone of that remark disturbed Bill even more than the affair that had occasioned it. *His* girl—as if he owned her! The boy turned gruffly to the sorry pair on the bank. "Get up and get out o' here," he ordered them. "You're lucky he didn't break your necks. Better stay clear o' the canal after this."

He stood over them with fists clenched, waiting for a sign of belligerence, but they had had all the fight taken out of them. Shakily they picked themselves up and stumbled off, muttering vague threats about bringing the town marshal.

When Bill went back aboard the *Tiger* Mary Ann was still sitting on the broad bench by the helm. Her hands lay listlessly in her lap and her face looked pale and sad in the twilight.

"Don't worry about it," he told her. " 'Twasn't your fault, and they got just what was coming to 'em."

When she made no answer he turned awkwardly and went back to his quarters in the stable.

If the two young men had any intention of bringing charges against Hoyle they evidently thought better of it. The night passed peacefully and the boat pulled out for the west next morning without interference from the law.

It was good farming country up there along the Ontario slope. Bill had expected to find an unsettled stretch of wilderness, but much of the land was already cleared and he saw flourishing young orchards and well-plowed fields. The towns were few and small but it was pleasant to wave to farmers toiling in the rich, dark soil.

Two days of steady hauling brought them to the foot of the long string of combines at Lockport. Bill had the team hitched before daylight so that the *Tiger* could be the first boat up, and when the sun rose they were past the locks, starting the final lap to Buffalo.

.   .   .   .

The morning of the twenty-fourth of April was bright and gay. A west wind off Lake Erie made the water dance in the canal at the foot of Buffalo docks. The *Tiger* had pulled in too late the night before for Bill to get much of a view of the city. Now he looked around him with a sense of pleasure. There was little beauty in the town itself. Everything was too new. Back from the docks ran whole streets of wooden houses that looked as if they had just been built and were still unfinished. The lumber was fresh and shining—unpainted but still unweathered. New board sidewalks ran along either side of rutted, raw highways. It was a boom town that had grown up with the brawling bustle of the canal.

Out to the west was the harbor. The masts of schooners stood high above the dockside buildings, and the blue lake reached away to the horizon. Everywhere big white birds that Bill thought must be gulls soared and sailed on lazy wings.

Buck Hoyle came out on deck and stretched his gorilla arms. "Come on, boy," he bellowed cheerfully. "Git yer breakfast in a hurry. We got to start unloadin' in twenty minutes."

Moving the *Tiger's* thirty-ton cargo was an all-day job for six men. Bill had never worked harder in his life than he did on that unloading. The hold was full of hoes, axes and spades, plowshares, sickles and scythes bound for the Michigan country. They were tied in neat bundles that were all a man could lift and carry. The boy found he could work as fast as any of the longshoremen, but keeping up with Buck Hoyle was beyond his powers. The burly canalman toiled like a steam engine and seemed as tireless.

When they lifted out the last of the freight Bill was wringing wet and his muscles ached with fatigue. It was four o'clock in the afternoon. He didn't know just when he would be paid off, but he went to the stable and collected his belongings, ready to leave.

Hoyle came back from the shipper's office about six, flourishing a roll of money. Evidently he had indulged in a few drinks already, but he was still sober enough to be in a good humor. Bill got up from the bunk where he had been resting when he heard the boater come to the stable door.

"Well, boy," Hoyle boomed, "ye done a good job o' drivin'. I'd be glad to keep ye on fer the trip back, but I reckon ye'll want to git along with yer peddlin'. Here's the five dollars I said I'd pay"

—he peeled some bills off the roll—"an' here's two dollars more fer the unloadin'—an' one that's a gift to spend on any foolishness ye want. Sleep aboard here tonight if ye ain't got no place else to go. Me—I'm aimin' to paint the town red!"

He guffawed mightily at that and his steely little eyes glittered with anticipation.

Bill took the money and thanked him. "Guess I'll move along tonight," he said. "I'm anxious to get on out to Ohio, where I'm headed."

Mary Ann called them to supper then. It was a good supper. Bill thought the girl must have taken special pains with it, knowing it would be a sort of farewell feast. The boater finished his food in haste and clapped his hat on his head. "Well, so long, young feller," he said. "I'm goin' to give Buffalo a treat. An' I'll be back with a present fer you, my gal, so don't make eyes at any boaters while I'm gone."

When he was off the boat Bill looked at Mary Ann. "Are you going to be here when he comes back?" he asked soberly.

She was pale and nervous but she tried to smile. "No," she said. "Don't worry about me, Bill.

There's a ship sailing before sunrise. I found out today while he was at work. I've already paid half my passage money and I'll have my things packed so I can leave after it gets dark."

"Gee," he told her, "that makes me feel better! Are you sure you've got enough money? He paid me a little extra, you know—"

"I've got plenty to get me to Cleveland," Mary Ann interrupted him. "You're nice to offer, though, Bill. Maybe I'll see you when we both get to Ohio. The place where my sister lives is called Buck Run. It's a little settlement with a grist-mill and a few farms, back in the woods."

Bill stood up and held out his hand. "I'll come, if I'm anywhere near there," he promised. "Now I'd better be going—so—good luck, Mary Ann!"

Their hands clasped quickly and then he turned, hurrying up the companion stairs. He slung the peddler's pack on his shoulders, gave the roans a farewell pat and stepped ashore, with Jody following close at his heels.

It did not take him long to reach the outskirts of the city, and a question or two put him on the turnpike leading south and west. Now, in the falling dusk, there was little traffic moving on the road. He tramped along in the broad ruts of the freight-wagons and saw the candle-light bloom in farmhouse windows.

Perhaps he hadn't realized how tired the day's work had made him. Before he had gone three miles from the city he found his head nodding and his feet stumbling. "Jody," he yawned, "I guess we'd better find a place to sleep."

Beyond the nearest pasture fence he could see a bushy clump of pine trees, dark against the sky. It was a warm, clear night—a good night for sleeping out of doors. Bill didn't bother with a fire, but scraped together a soft bed of pine-needles and lay down with his jacket wrapped around him. He was asleep so quickly and so soundly that it seemed only a moment before he sat up with the morning sun in his eyes.

Out on the road the dust was rising from plodding hoofs and creaking wheels. A big freight-wagon was going by, headed south. Bill put on his pack quickly. If he hurried he might get a lift.

As he climbed the fence several riders went past at a gallop, followed by two men in a chaise that

126

rattled along in a cloud of dust. He saw then that up and down the pike for a mile there were mounted men and vehicles, all hastening in the same direction. Whistling for Jody to follow, he set out after the freighter at a trot, the tin trunk jolting on his back.

The teamster was a jolly-looking little German with twinkling blue eyes in a round, pink face. He trudged beside his wheel-team, stepping very fast with his short legs to keep up with the long-striding horses.

"Sure," he answered Bill's question. "T'row yer leedle trunk up on der load in der back. Now ve talk, huh?"

Bill wasn't able to do much talking until he had caught his breath, but the German did not seem to mind. He jabbered away cheerfully while the boy tramped along at his side.

"Ve see der hanging, maybe, if ve go fast," he announced after a while.

"Hanging!" said Bill. "Is that what all these folks on the road are heading for?"

"Ja—sure. Und der's a auction, too. I buy me a hoss maybe, ja."

Bill wanted to know more, but at that moment they came over the brow of a low hill and saw a crowd of men gathered by the roadside. There was a little grove of trees there and horses and rigs of all kinds were tied in the shade. The teamster swung his leaders over on the grass and stopped the wagon at the edge of the crowd.

Suddenly Bill felt cold in spite of the morning sunshine. Before he turned his head away he had caught a glimpse of a long, dangling shadow, back there among the trees.

"I—I think I'll be goin' on," he told the German huskily.

But the little man caught his arm. "Look—der hosses!" he exclaimed. "Dem big blacks—dey're good ones, huh?" At the center of the milling circle of men, Bill saw an old buckboard with half a dozen horses hitched behind it. But it wasn't the big pair of blacks that made the boy stare. It was a rusty-coated, sleepy, old chestnut mare that stood beside them.

He stood on tiptoe, craning his neck to see more of the nags. There they were—the bony, string-halty gray—the solidly built Canada chunk—the slim, brown saddle-horse.

Bill gasped. He knew suddenly that Lon Peel would never rattle off that high-flown language of his again.

Up on the buckboard a big man stood, his hat pushed back to expose his bald and perspiring forehead. He placed one booted foot on the seat and shot a stream of tobacco-juice over the wheel.

"Now, gents," his flat voice brayed, "we got business to do here, an' time's a wastin'. This stock'll be auctioned off to the highest bidder, 'less'n some 'un kin prove ownership. Anybody claim any o' these hosses?"

"I do," called a voice from the crowd, and a brown-bearded man stepped forward. "Them blacks," he said, "was stole off my boat at Utica docks, ten nights back."

"Hold on, there," someone growled. "You got to prove it. I'm waitin' to bid on that there team."

"Yeah—he's right," others joined in. "You got to show us."

"My name's Ben Egan," the boater replied. "I'm well known on the canal. I hired relay hosses, when the blacks was stole, an' got in yesterday. I tell you that's my team."

The crowd was hostile now. "Go on, canawler—
you ain't proved nothin' yet!" they shouted.

Egan stood there with a baffled look in his eyes.
Then he went over to the horses. "Come, Dinty—
come, boy," he said soothingly, and reached up a
hand to stroke the nearer horse's neck. But the animal jerked away nervously. Unkind laughter rose
from the bystanders. "Hey, Mike," one called.
"Chase this feller out an' let's start the biddin'."

Bill never knew just how he got there, but the
next moment he found himself at Egan's side. "I
was in Utica when you lost 'em," he told the boater
hurriedly. "And what's more I know Lon Peel was
there that night. I saw him!"

Ben Egan gaped at him, a look of relief gradually spreading over his face. "Gosh, boy!" he said.
"I don't remember you, but, by gum, if it's true
what you're sayin' it ought to help. Step up there
an' tell 'em what ye know."

Bill had to swallow once or twice before he
could speak. That ring of hard, unfriendly faces
was not a very encouraging audience. But once he
got started he told his story convincingly.

"Wait a minute!" someone called. "Ye say ye know Peel by sight. What makes ye think this hoss-thief we ketched was the same feller?"

Bill thought a minute, then had an inspiration. "If it's Peel," he said, "you ought to find a queer contraption in his duffel, there on the buckboard —a thing with pictures painted on it an' little white buttons on the side."

The big auctioneer rummaged among the horse-thief's belongings. "By ding!" he said, lifting the accordion gingerly. "Looks like the boy's right. What in tarnation is it, anyhow?"

"He used to make music with it," Bill answered. "Like this"—and he reached up for the instrument. Fumbling with eager fingers he undid the strap that held it closed, pressed down a couple of the stops and pulled the bellows open. The high, wailing note that burst forth made the bystanders jump back, treading on each other's toes.

The man on the buckboard raised his hand. "I'm satisfied," he shouted above the hubbub. "Egan, you kin keep yore hosses till we git some more evidence from boaters that knows you. Now, gents, quiet while we proceed with the biddin'!"

CHAPTER

THE better horses were led out first and the auctioneer went to work. He bellowed the praises of each animal till he was red in the face and paused only to mop his head with a bandanna handkerchief. The bidding was spirited. The brown saddle-horse brought a final figure of $140,

TEN

and the Canada drafter was knocked down for
$105. At the end of an hour the only horses left
at the buckboard tail were the feeble gray nag and
the old mare. The spectators began to leave and the
little German nudged Bill. "Ve go on, huh? Nod-
dings more here dot's any goot," he said.

But Bill shook his head. "Thanks for the lift," he told the teamster, "but I reckon I'll wait a little. Maybe I'll catch up to you this afternoon."

He couldn't have said just why he stayed. Perhaps he was sorry for the two ancient beasts. There was some ribald laughter as the gray was led out at a stumbling trot.

"Two shillin'!" somebody said.

The auctioneer grinned. It was no use wasting breath on this one. "Shucks," he said, "his hide's worth a dollar. Do I hear a dollar? One dollar I got—gimme two—gimme two. Dollar an' a half—lemme hear six bits—dollar an' a half—any more bids? Goin' at one an' a half. One an' a half once—twice—an' sold to the gent in the butternut breeches!"

The gray's owner stepped out sheepishly and led his new purchase away, and the rusty-coated mare was untied from the buckboard. Looking at her gentle face and the docile way she followed at the end of her halter, Bill knew what he had waited for.

"Now here's a good old lady," the auctioneer joked. "Fair, fat an' forty—not a day more. Somebody gimme a bid an’ let’s git this over. Who’ll say ten dollars?”

“Five dollars!” Bill hardly recognized his own voice.

“Six,” said a man on the other side of the crowd.

“Six an’ a half,” Bill answered.

“Seven.” The man’s voice was indifferent.

Bill counted up his assets with fumbling fingers. His total cash amounted to $9.80.

“Eight dollars!” he called with a boldness he was far from feeling.

“Nine,” the other bidder replied sardonically, and the crowd laughed. Bill’s face reddened and he was starting to turn away when another man spoke at his elbow. It was Ben Egan, the boater. “Ten dollars,” he said.

At that the auctioneer’s enthusiasm returned. “Now we’re gettin’ somewhere,” he bawled. “Come on, gents—ten I got—who’ll gimme twelve?”

But no amount of persuasion brought another bid. The man on the other side of the circle had lost interest and strolled away.

“Goin’ at ten, once,” came the call from the buckboard. “Goin’ twice—three times—an’ gone,

to our friend the canawler with the brown whis-
kers."

"Gee," said Bill, "I'm glad 'twas you that got
her, Mr. Egan. I reckon you know how to treat
horses."

"Me?" the boater grinned. "No, son, that mare's
yourn. I could see you wanted her, an' by gum I
ain't one to fergit a favor!"

Bill stood by speechless while Egan handed the
money to the auctioneer and took the mare's halter. He was still staring in unbelief when the
boater held out the end of the rope to him.

"Go on, youngster—take her," Egan chuckled.
"Ten dollars is a mighty cheap price to pay fer gittin' my team back."

"Gosh!" Bill breathed at last. "I never thought
you were—gosh! I dunno how to thank you! But
I'll sure take good care of her!"

He found his pack, where the German had left
it by the roadside, and put it on his shoulders. Five
minutes later he was marching down the turnpike
with the mare plodding behind him and Jody trotting importantly ahead. In the last three weeks, the
boy thought with a grin, he had acquired quite a

family.

At a cross-roads store, two or three miles down the road, he dickered for a length of rope and tied the pack on the mare's back. "Old lady," he told her, "you'll carry that a lot easier than I can, an' you've got to earn your keep. Let's see—what was it Peel called you? Martha—that's the name. Nice an' gentle. It sort of suits you. I've got an idea he thought quite a lot o' you, from the way he talked. It wasn't because he was soft-hearted like me, either. Wonder what he saw in you, Martha?"

So he conversed with the mare as they tramped along, and though she didn't answer him in words, her wise brown eyes looked at him with friendly understanding.

Bill did not cover as much ground as he had expected that afternoon. Old Martha's pace was slow and, not knowing when she had been fed, he stopped several times to let her graze on the roadside grass. At the store he had replenished his stock of bacon, corn meal and tea so that he would not be dependent on eating at farmhouses. Now, as evening approached, he began looking around for a likely place to make camp.

The little cavalcade was on a lonely stretch of road, shadowed by dark woods on either side. At the bottom of a little hollow Bill saw a rivulet coming down from the left. It was only a yard or two across at its widest part, but it offered a promise of good water. He was about to turn into the woods beside the stream when he heard a patter of feet on the road.

"Bill!" called a breathless voice. Running toward him down the hill he was amazed to see the girl Mary Ann, her black hair disheveled and her dress torn.

She could hardly speak for panting when she reached his side, but she seized his arm and urged him toward the shelter of the woods. "Hoyle!" she managed to gasp at last. "I'm scared, Bill! Maybe he's—he's following me!"

The girl was so exhausted it was all she could do to stand. Surprised as he was at seeing her there, Bill knew this was no time for questions. He half lifted, half pulled her through the brambles and in a few moments they were hidden from the road. Bill tied the mare to a tree. When he turned back to Mary Ann he found her sobbing into a wet ball of handkerchief. He didn't know much about girls but after one or two ineffectual efforts to comfort her he decided the best thing to do was to leave her alone.

In a narrow ravine beyond the trees he built a small fire and started water heating. When the bacon and johnnycake were ready and tea was steeping in the little kettle he looked up to see the girl standing beside him. She had stopped crying and was trying to smile.

"I guess I'm silly, Bill," she said, "but I was so tired! I left Buffalo around noon and got one short lift on a farmer's wagon. I've been running and walking as fast as I could ever since—trying to catch up with you."

"Here—sit down," he urged. "Lean up against the tree there and I'll give you some supper."

She obeyed with a meekness that surprised him. All her saucy independence was gone, for the time at least, and she was just a weary, hungry youngster, glad to have someone take care of her. When she had finished the meal she told him her story.

She had left the *Mohawk Tiger* about one o'clock the night before, carrying her belongings in a bag made of an old skirt and trusting to the cover of the darkness along the docks.

The schooner was crowded with emigrants and she was told she would have to share a bunk in the narrow public cabin with another woman. She had crawled into bed and was trying to go to sleep when there came an uproar on the deck and Buck Hoyle stormed into the cabin, drunk and ugly. He dragged her from the berth and off the ship, knocking two of the sailors out of his path. Back at the canal-boat he threw her down the companion-steps and locked the door. Then he stretched himself on the deck outside.

"When he was snoring," Mary Ann said, "I tried both the windows. One was nailed shut and the other was too small to get through. I waited all morning—I'm afraid I cried some—because I'd lost my passage money and my spare clothes. Finally, around noon, Hoyle woke up and went up to the tavern again. I just had to get out some way. So I took the kindling-wood hatchet and chopped the lock off the door. I waited till there was a farm wagon going by and walked along beside it so Hoyle couldn't see me from the bar. When I got to the corner I asked the farmer for a ride and he brought me two or three miles. The rest of the way I've come afoot."

She smiled at him wanly as she pulled off one of her shoes and displayed a red blister on her heel.

Bill brought the skillet from the fire. "Here," he said. "You fixed me up with mutton tallow once. Maybe bacon grease would help. Gosh, Mary Ann, I'm glad you got away, even if you did lose everything!"

He sat for a while, chin in hands, staring into the dying embers of the fire. It was dark now, and he could barely see the silent girl beside him.

"I've been figuring," he said at last. "You think Hoyle'll follow you, an' I expect you're right. But the closer we are to Buffalo, the easier he can find you. So we ought to keep moving, and the time to do it is at night. You can ride my mare"—he said the words with a certain pride—"an' we can make a lot o' distance before daylight. Then we'll hide out till it's dark again."

He got up and collected the utensils and provisions. Old Martha seemed a little surprised when he strapped the folded blanket on her back, but she followed obediently while he led her to the brook and watered her. A few minutes later they were moving warily down the dark road.

Bill walked along by the mare's head, his pack on his back once more, and as they went he told Mary Ann about the hanging of Lon Peel and the luck that had made him Martha's owner.

There was little travel on the pike that night. Once they turned hastily into a lane as the mail-coach to the south went clattering by. And once, when they heard the swift gallop of a single horse, Bill pulled the mare into the middle of a thicket till the rider passed. For a moment they thought it might be Hoyle, but as he drew away down the road they heard him singing in a high tenor voice that could never have come from the big boater's throat.

Mary Ann rode until her head was nodding with sleep, then climbed down and trudged at Bill's side. She didn't complain, and much as Bill hated to do it he kept the little procession moving doggedly on till the east began to gray and roosters crowed in distant farmyards. They must have covered fifteen miles before morning.

As the first light came through the trees the boy saw a grass-grown wagon track leading into the woods on the right, and at the end of it, fifty yards from the pike, a roughly built log cabin.

"Might as well go in there," he told the drowsy girl. "It's pretty much out o' sight from the road, an' soon as the folks are up they'll give us some breakfast. Gosh—you *are* tired, aren't you?"

He caught her arm as she was about to topple off the mare's broad back. He had to shake her to make her open her eyes. There were no fresh tracks in the path they followed toward the cabin. The young grass had sprung up with no foot to trample it. So Bill was not surprised to see the shack's door hanging from one broken hinge and the roof sagging in the middle. He went to the door and looked in. The single room was empty except for a drifted heap of dry leaves on the earth floor. A chipmunk popped its head out of a hole under the eaves and scolded him for a moment before it whisked out of sight.

The boy lifted Mary Ann down and carried her into the deserted house. She was too exhausted to care where she slept but he made her as comfortable as he could with the blanket laid over the pile of leaves. Then he tethered the mare behind the shack and set about getting a meal. There was a path through the near-by undergrowth and as he expected it led to a spring, choked with weeds but full of clear water. He brought a kettleful back to the cabin and built a fire on the baked clay hearth. At the end of half an hour he had prepared a breakfast of sorts.

Mary Ann still slept and he hadn't the heart to wake her. Counting back he realized that this was the first real sleep she had had since the night they docked in Buffalo. He ate his own food, doused the fire and tied Jody inside the shack. Then he lay down across the open door. He was pretty tired himself. So tired that in a few seconds he was slumbering as soundly as his companion.

It was a sudden spring shower beating in on his face that woke him, late in the afternoon. The sun shone through the slant bars of rain and glistened on young leaves and grass. Behind him in the gloom of the cabin he heard the little hound whimper softly and the girl stirred, rustling her leaf bed. She was sitting up, rubbing her eyes when he turned.

"Hungry?" he asked with a grin.

"Mmm," she said sleepily. "I guess that's what's the matter with me. What time is it?"

"Round about four, I reckon. I'll hustle up some grub in a minute."

"No, let me—I'm feeling ever so much better. Just show me where the provisions are."

Bill built a fire and brought more water from the spring, then sat down in comfort while Mary Ann went about getting their supper. She was just turning the golden brown johnnycake out of the pan when Bill heard a sound. He lifted a finger to his lips and went quietly to the door. There was a horse coming down the road—a heavy horse coming at a gallop.

As the thunder of hoofs grew louder Bill crouched, his hand over Jody's muzzle. He had caught a flying glimpse of the horse through the half-bare branches and it was a red roan, dark with sweat and flecked with lather.

CHAPTER

"IS it—is it him?" came Mary Ann's scared whisper.

Bill nodded, pointing where a gap in the trees promised a momentary view of the rider. There he went—a hulking brute of a man, slouched forward in the saddle, his great shoulders and black

146

ELEVEN

hair wet from the recent rain.

"Yes," said Bill slowly. "It's him all right. An' the way he's pushing old Prince, he's plenty mad. Maybe we'll have to stay hid instead o' moving on tonight."

They doused the fire, making sure there was no

more smoke coming from the chimney, and ate their supper in silence.

"Bill," said Mary Ann after a while, "I'm likely to get you in trouble if I stay with you. I'm all right, now I've had some rest, and I could make out to get along by myself."

Bill frowned. "How could you?" he asked. "You've got no grub and mighty little money. You can't sleep out in those clothes if it should turn cold. An' there's plenty o' tough characters in this part o' the country. Anyhow, you can't start off now, with Hoyle somewhere down the road ahead of you."

The evening was mild and clear after the shower. They sat in the doorway of the shack and watched the sun go down and the light fade in the sky. It was growing dusk when they heard the sound of hoofs on the road again. A long time passed before the horse came abreast of them, for it was moving at a tired walk. The boy and girl had crept inside, where they could peer out without betraying their presence.

Bill stared at the spent horse. "Poor old Prince," he whispered. "He's sure done in. Look at him stumble."

But Mary Ann was watching the huge, slumped figure of the man in the saddle. She shivered a little. "I think if he knew I was here—the way he feels now," she breathed, "he'd beat the living daylights out of me."

They waited till the last sound of plodding hoofs had died away to the northward, then packed up and set out once more on their journey. At the girl's insistence Bill loaded his trunk on old Martha's back. She was as well able to walk as he was, she told him.

A young moon gave them light for the first few miles, and after it had set they tramped on, guiding their footsteps by the sandy track that was a shade or two lighter than the surrounding darkness. It was a lonely stretch of country, with few clearings. Off in the deep woods they heard owls hooting dolefully and once a wildcat screamed, so near that Jody came cowering against Bill's legs. The boy and girl walked close together, silent but glad of each other's company.

After five or six hours they rested beside a brook and ate the handful of cold johnnycake that Mary Ann had saved from their supper. When dawn came Bill found a camping place in the woods some distance from the road. After they had cooked and eaten breakfast he left the girl there with the mare, and walked on alone to reconnoiter what looked like a settlement half a mile ahead.

There were eight or ten houses clustered around a little frame church, a cross-roads store and a blacksmith shop. In front of the smithy was a big four-horse freight-wagon with one wheel off. The teamster was sitting on a nail-keg by the door, smoking his pipe while the smith repaired the broad iron tire.

"Mornin'," he nodded as Bill passed. "You ain't by any chance a peddler, be you, lad?"

"Why, yes," Bill replied in some surprise, for he was not carrying his pack.

The freighter squinted at him a moment and spat thoughtfully. "Guess you ain't the one," he said. "There was a rough customer on the road last night lookin' fer a boy 'bout your age. Said his cook had run off with him. But you don't 'pear to have no gal 'long of you."

Bill mustered up a grin. "No," he answered. "I guess he's after somebody else."

He thought fast while he was walking on toward the store and by the time he reached the board platform in front of the building, a plan had formed in his mind.

The store was dark and musty, lighted only by one square window in the front. Its small interior was crowded with all sorts of merchandise, from hams and crackers and molasses to harness, boots and hardware. At the sound of Bill's step the storekeeper appeared from the back room, still munching the last of his breakfast.

Bill asked for three pounds of corn meal. While it was being weighed out he looked along the dusty shelves till he found what he wanted.

"Got a pair o' blue jean breeches to fit me?" he asked carelessly.

"Shouldn't wonder," said the merchant. "Them's extry solid ones. Sell fer a dollar 'n' two bits."

"Let's look at 'em."

The boy held a pair of the breeches in front of him as if measuring the waist band. "Might be a shade large," he said, "but that's better than having 'em too tight. All right, I'll give you a dollar."

After a little dickering they agreed on a dollar and one shilling, with the corn meal thrown in. "Wrap 'em up together in a piece o' paper," said Bill. And with the package under his arm he returned whistling past the blacksmith shop.

All was peaceful at the little camping place. Martha and Jody had both lain down to sleep, and Mary Ann was mending the rent in her skirt with a needle and thread taken from Bill's pack.

"You're not going to need that skirt for a while," the boy told her with a chuckle. "Look what I got for you."

He undid the bundle and held up the blue jeans.

"Why, Bill!" she blushed. "You know I'd be ashamed. Men's pantaloons! What an idea!"

But when he told her about his encounter with the teamster she changed her mind. "I could cut off my hair," she said doubtfully. "But are you sure they'd take me for a boy?"

"Why not? Let's hear you talk in a deep voice— deep as you can."

She practiced a little, laughing at her own efforts, and at length Bill was satisfied. "You won't have to say much, anyhow," he told her. "And your voice would pass for a boy about fifteen. I hate to see you lose that pretty black hair, but it's got to be done, I reckon. You can wear my hat and jacket and ride the mare. Nobody that Hoyle has talked to knows I've got her. We'll wait till afternoon and then start along, with you riding on ahead so we won't be seen together till we're clear o' the town."

Mary Ann retired behind a pine thicket and put on the blue jeans. Then her hair was cropped off at the neck-line with a pair of Bill's trade scissors. In the homespun jacket and broad-brimmed hat she looked so much like a fresh-faced country lad that Bill himself hardly recognized her.

They rested a few hours, ate a meal and made ready for the road. The girl climbed gaily aboard old Martha and rode off with a wave to Bill. "Don't worry," she said. "You can look for me down the pike a way."

When she had been gone twenty minutes Bill strapped on his pack, called Jody, and started after her. The village dozed in the warm sun of early afternoon. The wagon was gone from in front of the smithy and the only living thing he saw as he passed along the dusty road was an old black dog drowsing on the store platform. It opened one eye to look at Jody but decided the effort of scraping an acquaintance would be too great.

Two miles beyond the settlement Bill came over a rise and saw the mare browsing contentedly by the roadside, but he looked in vain for the boyish figure of Mary Ann. When he reached the place he called once or twice without getting an answer. Old Martha's halter was tied to a sapling. He undid the granny knot and stood undecided, wondering where the girl could have gone.

"Come, Jody," he coaxed. "You ought to be a good trailer. Which way did she go?"

The little hound wagged his tail eagerly, put his nose to the ground and sniffed in a slow circle. On the hard ground at the edge of the road he came to a stop, whimpered a little and looked up at his master.

"Shucks," said Bill, "you're no help at all."

Worried now, he turned back to the mare and saw a scrap of white paper peeping out from a fold of the saddle blanket. Quickly he pulled it forth and read the words scribbled on it.

"I'm going on alone," it said. "I would not want anything to happen to you and I will be all

right. Am sorry to take the coat and hat but will return them or pay for them when I get to Ohio. Thank you for everything."

Bill was so surprised that he sat down heavily on the bank. He admired the girl's spunk but after having appointed himself her protector it took the wind out of his sails to have her go off like this. And when he thought of the long distance that lay ahead he was afraid of what might happen to her.

Maybe, he thought, if he hurried he could still overtake her. She couldn't be much more than a mile ahead. But when he sprang up and started to urge the mare forward he realized that speed was out of the question. Martha was willing enough, but try as he would, he could not get her to move faster than an ambling walk.

There was nothing for it but to go ahead at the old mare's moderate gait. He marched along, inwardly fuming, his eyes always searching the road as far as he could see it. A freight-wagon creaked up behind him, its big horses stepping fast through the cloud of dust they raised. The driver nodded as they pulled by. Bill wondered if Mary Ann would risk asking some of these passing teamsters for a ride.

He plodded on through the afternoon and halted only when darkness came. It was a lonesome business cooking breakfast next morning with only himself and Jody to eat it. Gradually, however, as the day wore on he recovered some of his good spirits. He was in better farming country now. He passed acre after acre of well-pruned apple orchards and stump pastures where sheep and lambs were grazing. At noon he stopped at a farmhouse for dinner. The farmer's wife welcomed him with joy when she saw his pack. "A peddler!" she cried. "I been wantin' a few things the worst way but the men-folks are too busy to go to town fer 'em."

While Bill ate she continued her chatter. "I heard there was a peddler on the road an' might be along soon," she told him. "A young lad come by here last night an' my husband let him sleep in the barn. He mentioned havin' passed you earlier."

Bill put down his knife. "That right?" he asked, trying to keep his tone casual. "Wonder who it could have been."

"Don't know as I recollect hearin' the boy's name," she replied. "But he was a nice-lookin', black-haired youngster, dressed sort of outlandish. Said he was goin' out to Ohio to see his kinfolks."

As soon as Bill finished eating he opened his trunk on the long kitchen table. The woman was in a flutter trying to decide between a gilt brooch and a pair of red glass ear-rings—then choosing a shade of braid to trim a new dress. It took two hours for her to complete her selections but at the end of that time she gave Bill two dollars and some change in payment for what she had bought.

"I'm luckier'n some women that way," she told him. "It's my chicken an' egg money. My husband lets me keep it fer gewgaws like this."

He went on his way well satisfied with his afternoon's work and glad to have had news of Mary Ann. For he had no doubt about the identity of the "black-haired youngster" who had slept in the barn the night before. She was making good time —far ahead of him by now. He wondered if she had intended that he should get the message when she mentioned having seen him.

Bill stopped at two or three more farmhouses before dark, but he came across no such eager customers as the first one. One woman offered to trade a bushel of shriveled potatoes for a length of calico, but couldn't spare a sack to put them in. As he was soon to discover, the farther west he went the harder it was to find cash.

It rained that night, but he got shelter in the cowshed of a farmer who gave him supper and breakfast for his help with the chores. He set out again in the chill of a wet morning, wishing he had his jacket. Then he remembered that it was probably raining on Mary Ann too and wrapped his blanket around him without regrets.

So he plodded hour after hour down the muddy road and paid no heed to the jibes of passing teamsters. By noon it showed signs of clearing. A fresh southwesterly breeze sprang up and the blanket was dry when he stopped at dusk in a grove where the road forded a shallow river.

There was no longer any need for him to hide. He led the mare to an open glade among the trees overlooking the ford and made camp.

A couple of farm-wagons jolted by on their way home from market. The Erie stage went careening through the water with a splash of hoofs and a squeal or two from the lady passengers. Then the quiet of the spring night descended and Bill lay down with his feet to the fire.

He had been sleeping soundly for a long time when Jody's growl woke him. The little hound was cowering against him, shivering as if scared half out of his wits. Bill sat up cautiously, rubbing his eyes and listening. From somewhere across the river a confused low murmur of sound came to him. It grew louder—a throbbing beat of many hoofs—a groaning of wheels. Then he saw lights winking and bobbing between the tree-stems. A man shouted sleepily at a team. And a queer, unrecognizable, animal smell drifted past.

Bill rose hastily and crept forward to the edge of the grove. Jody whimpered but came with him. And behind him the boy could hear old Martha snorting and fidgeting at her tether.

He could see the road now, and the rippling water, with a yellow path on it made by the setting moon. There were dim, huge shapes moving on the other side of the river. One of the lights he had glimpsed came down to the edge of the ford and he saw it was a smoking torch held by a man on mule-back. The mule put its nose down to drink, then came splashing across. But it was not the mule or its rider that held Bill's petrified gaze. It was the beast that followed—dark, gigantic, swaying forward with vast, deliberate strides. In the uncertain light of the torches it looked bigger than a barn.

He had never seen an elephant except in pictures, but he knew he was looking at one now.

BILL scarcely breathed while the elephant waded the stream and came up the road. Its swinging trunk curled to and fro like a hungry snake, and as it passed him the exploring tip nearly touched his face. Then without a sound the great beast moved on.

TWELVE

It was a strange procession that followed. The crouching boy watched one big wagon after another toil through the ford and scramble up the nearer bank. In the flare of the torches he could see red paint and fat gilt cupids on their sides. Others were open, with moonlight shining through their iron bars, and it wasn't until two or three of these had passed that he saw big, furry shapes huddled in the cages and caught the pungent cat-reek that came from them. He had to hold Jody's muzzle to keep the frightened little dog from whimpering.

Bill didn't try to count the wagons. There must have been nearly a score of them, each pulled by a four-horse team. When the last one creaked away into the darkness, the boy stood up slowly and drew a long breath. "Gee whillikers!" he whispered in awe. "You know what we've just seen, Jody? A real, honest-to-goodness travelin' circus!"

He went back to his blanket then, but it was a long time before he could get to sleep.

. . . .

It took Bill two more days of tramping to reach the border of New York State. His attempts to sell his goods along the road met with little success and after a few fruitless calls he decided to wait till he reached the real backwoods. Meanwhile he kept his face to the southwest and walked from dawn till dark.

According to his reckoning it was the first day

of May when he towed old Martha into the town of Erie. All morning he had been sniffing a spring breeze from the south, heavy with the scent of apple-blossoms.

The old lake port was busy with wagons and shipping. Word had gone forth that the ice was out of the Detroit River, and families by the score were flocking toward homestead lands in the brand new state of Michigan.

Bill plodded down the noisy main street toward a big, comfortable-looking tavern. The wide yard was flanked by stables, and a sign that swung from the front of the building bore the words, "Teamsters' Rest." There was an air of cheery welcome about the place that was irresistible. Bill led the mare in between a couple of towering "mountain-ships"—the covered wagons that hauled freight over the Pennsylvania hills.

"Give her a stall and a bait of grain," he told the hostler at the stable door. "I won't be moving on till I've had dinner."

In the tavern dining-room, Bill gave himself the luxury of ordering the things he had been hankering for all down the road from Buffalo. A big slice of juicy roast beef—mashed potatoes and gravy—white bread and butter and plum preserves. The waitress who set his heaping plate before him looked speculatively from the bareheaded boy to the peddler's pack behind his chair.

"Your name," she said saucily, "wouldn't be Bill Crawford, would it?"

He looked up in surprise. "Why, sure," he said. "How'd you know?"

She laughed and dimpled. "Oh, a little bird told me," she replied, and switched away to the kitchen.

He wondered at her knowing his name but it did not curb his hearty appetite. Twenty minutes later, when she handed him his pie, the puzzle was solved. "There was someone stopped here a day or two ago," the girl teased. "Said you'd likely be along soon, an' I was to give you a parcel."

"A parcel?"

"Yeah. I've put it there with your pack."

He looked quickly behind him. It was his homespun jacket, blue jeans, and old broad-brimmed hat, tied in a bundle with butcher's string.

"Thanks," Bill stammered. "Was she—was she

making out all right?"

But the waitress was gone.

Bill finished his pie and paid for his dinner. Back in the stable with his pack and the parcel, he found a private corner behind the grain-bins and untied the string. As he had half expected, there was a bit of paper folded into the coat. Opening it he read the message written in Mary Ann's round hand.

"Dear Bill," it said. "All through that rain I kept wishing you had these to wear. I hope you did not take your death of cold. When I got here I washed dishes for a meal and one of the hired girls has been very good to me. She got me some proper woman's clothes, so I can now return the ones you gave me. I expect you will come here to eat when you get to Erie, because it is full of horses and I know that is the kind of place you like. If you do not come along in the next week my friend has promised to send the bundle on to me by the next boat that sails. So I guess you will get the clothes one way or the other."

It was signed, "Faithfully yours, Mary Ann Bennett."

Bill put on the hat and tied the other garments with his pack. He was glad to get his clothes back but he wished the girl had told him more about her journey. He knew she was making good progress—probably getting lifts from passing teamsters. Maybe she would be better off without her disguise. She could take care of herself, as she had frequently told him.

Bill paid for the mare's oats and strapped the pack on her broad back. "Come on, old lady," he coaxed her, "we've got to get along or we'll never reach Ohio."

On the broad road that led out of Erie to the west, there were crowds moving, in vehicles, on horseback and afoot. A brisk, wiry little man with flowing white hair came by, walking at a smart pace, and Bill asked him where everybody was heading.

"Hoss-race," the oldster replied. "Out to the fair-grounds track. Ain't ye heard? They's a purse o' five hundred dollars fer the best trotter under saddle, an' a couple o' 'York State hosses is entered. We got some goers right 'round here that'll make 'em step, though. Can't ye git that mare to go any faster? Ye'll be missin' the start."

The long oval of the track was in sight now and Bill urged the mare forward in an effort to keep alongside the old man. "Who do you think'll win?" he asked.

"Ain't a sayin'. Squire Mason's Black Eagle's powerful fast, but he mightn't be able to stay fer four mile. Cap'n Couder's got a little brown mare that's a flash. Then again this 'York Stater, Tomahawk, is s'posed to be almighty good."

"I heard about him back in Troy," Bill put in eagerly. "He's a son of Onondaga Chief, an' he trotted in two-thirty-six last fall when he was just a four-year-old."

The old man sniffed, as much as to say some of these youngsters were too smart for their own good. "All the watches is slow in 'York State when it comes to timin' hosses," he commented drily.

They were pushing through the crowd now. Bill hitched the mare when he found an opening along the fence, and he and his white-haired friend hurried over to the track-side.

The oval had been marked out on a broad, level meadow. Only the worn, trampled turf and a row of stakes along the inside of each curve showed where it ran.

"That there's a measured half mile," the old fellow explained. "They'll go 'round eight times. Look yonder—the riders is gittin' up now."

Bill saw half a dozen horses in the middle of a knot of spectators. One after another the jockeys swung into their saddles and as the crowd scattered, the trotters came out, prancing and pawing.

They made a pretty sight. There was a big black horse with a gleaming coat and a fiery eye—Squire Mason's mount, the old man said. The captain's mare was small and neatly built, with a dainty, nervous head and smooth action. Among the others Bill had no difficulty in picking out the son of the famous Onondaga Chief. Tomahawk was not a very big horse but he was put together with a compact beauty that would take any knowing horseman's eye. His coat was a rich, ruddy chestnut and he had a fine white star in his forehead. The only other white on him was a pair of flashing white "stockings" reaching from his front hoofs halfway to the knee.

The riders sat straight as ramrods in their saddles and rode with a long stirrup. Some wore only their bright waistcoats, breeches and boots, while others—the stout Squire Mason among them— were in the full regalia of skirted broadcloth coats and beaver hats.

There were shouts of encouragement from the crowd as the racers limbered up their muscles in short practice trots out across the meadow and back.

A bull-voiced man was bellowing orders. "Ready, gentlemen?" he roared. "Take 'em around once to get the feel o' the course. Bring 'em down even to the line an' I'll fire one shot to give you a start."

The jockeys seemed to pay little attention to his advice. For several more minutes each went his own way till he was satisfied his mount was properly warmed up. Then they began assembling in a more or less orderly group near the starting line.

"All right—take one lap easy and come around for a fair start," bawled the loud-voiced official.

There was some rearing and cavorting and one or two of the more nervous horses tried to bolt, but after a moment all six got away in reasonably good order. The riders held them to an ordinary road pace around the first turn and down the back stretch. Then, on the far turn, some of them let out a notch. They were all picking up speed as they came down toward the line, the mettlesome black pulling away from the pack by two or three lengths.

But though the cries of the crowd expressed disapproval the starter seemed to think it was as good a start as he was likely to get. He lifted his pistol in the air and the report barked across the meadow.

Bill leaned forward, tense with excitement, yelling with the rest. The horses had settled down to trot. Their spirited heads were lowered, their legs flashed rhythmically, and their tails streamed out in the wind.

For the first mile and a half the big black horse held his comfortable lead unchallenged. Then, early in the fourth lap, the other riders began jockeying for position. Content till now to hold their places, one after another gave his horse its head and made a bid for the lead. It was the captain's mare that first replaced Black Eagle on the pole. She moved out like a little brown steam-engine and her rush carried the black into a break. He galloped a hundred yards while the squire sawed at his mouth, trying to pull him back to the gait, and by the time he was trotting again all but one of the contenders had passed him.

Bill's eyes were on Tomahawk. The chestnut moved so easily that he hardly seemed to be trying, but his rider had kept him well up with the leaders. It was not until the horses were rounding the far turn on the seventh lap that the star-faced trotter put on speed. Bill saw him coming wide out of the turn, his head and tail level, his clean legs moving square and true.

Tomahawk's rider was leaning forward now as if he wanted to talk into the chestnut's ear. They flew down the stretch and into the last half mile with the brown mare still clinging to the lead and the 'York State horse close on her flank. It was a race between these two now, for all the others were many lengths behind.

On the back stretch Captain Couder began to use his whip. The game little mare responded with an effort that kept her in front till they had rounded the last turn. Then she could hold the pace no longer. Tomahawk's white star came blazing into the lead. Faster and faster flew his hoofs. There was no whipping needed for that final surge of speed. He was trotting for the pure joy of doing his best.

Even the jealous loyalty of the Pennsylvanians could not keep them from bursting into a spontaneous cheer. Bill shouted with the men around him till his throat was hoarse, and the old man beside him forgot local pride in his excitement.

"That," he stated, when the hubbub had quieted down, "is the best gol-dinged trotter I ever see. Yessir, the plumb best. Ye got to admit, though, the little mare give him somethin' to think about."

Together they worked their way into the dense crowd of spectators that had gathered around the victor and the judges. The rider of the chestnut was still in the saddle—a florid, laughing young man with a reckless look in his blue eyes.

"It gives me great pleasure," the bull-voiced judge announced, "to hand this purse o' five hundred dollars to Mr. Merrick o' New York. A fine race, sir—an' a fine horse."

He held up his hand as the cheers broke out again. "The time," he shouted, "was eleven minutes an' eight seconds—the fastest four miles ever trotted west o' the Allegheny Mountains!"

There were more yells of acclaim, then young Mr. Merrick swung down from Tomahawk's back and led him out through the press of bystanders. Bill was so close that he could reach out and touch the glistening chestnut flank as the horse went by.

"Gosh!" he murmured. "He isn't even breathing hard!" He turned to the old man with eyes that were alight. "If I could own a horse like that some day," he said, "I'd rather have him than a million dollars!"

CHAPTER

A DAY'S journey beyond Erie brought
Bill to a country that grew more primi-
tive as he advanced. The prosperous,
well-cleared farms he had passed on the way down
from Buffalo were gone now. In their place he
encountered miles of rolling hills, wooded with

THIRTEEN

oak and beech and butternut, maple and ash and hickory. Even the latest of the hardwoods were coming into leaf, and the morning light shone on a sea of tender green varied with a hundred hues and shadings.

Occasionally he would come to a little settlement where half a dozen homesteads had been cleared and the log houses were all in sight of each other, as if for company. He was getting close to Ohio now.

When it was that he actually crossed the line he did not know. But on the morning of the fourth of May, when he stopped to ask a farmer for a drink of well-water, the man told him he had been traveling through Ohio for miles.

The road had degenerated into a broad, winding track, trampled into the earth by horses and cattle, dotted in places with stumps, broken wagon wheels and refuse left by the "movers." Bill passed some of them that day—slow caravans of ox-teams pulling patched-up wagons. There were young couples starting out to build their first homes in the northern counties or Indiana. And there were whole families—lean, bearded men with restless eyes, tired-looking women and barefooted children of assorted ages—shifting westward in the hope of finding a living on new soil. They carried with them everything they possessed. Under the tattered wagon-covers were stacked their furniture, bedding, cookstoves, chicken-coops, guns, plows and farming-implements.

There was no hurrying the oxen. If a mover's wagon made fifteen miles between sunrise and sunset it was a long day's journey. From Pennsylvania to Michigan or Illinois might take two weary months.

Sometimes the boy tramped alongside, chatting with the emigrant families. But the painful slowness of the cattle was more than he could stand for any length of time. Even Martha's gentle pace seemed swift compared to the snail-like gait of the oxen.

Once or twice Bill made small sales to the more prosperous movers, but for the most part they were too poor to do any trading. It was at the log homesteads along the road that he now started his peddling in earnest. At first he had felt a certain awkwardness about knocking at a door and offering his wares, but he soon began to enjoy it.

He found that if he smiled and spoke cheerfully the householders were usually glad to welcome him in. The men asked him questions about affairs back East. As one who had recently come from such populous centers as Buffalo and Erie, they considered him a sort of oracle on the news of the day.

The women were almost pathetically eager to see and finger the trinkets in his pack. Often they had no money with which to buy, but he was developing a system of barter. There was nearly always some article of home manufacture that his customers were willing to trade for what they wanted. Bill, who knew little about the prices such things would bring in the towns, accepted only what he was sure he could sell. By the time he had traveled a few miles beyond Ashtabula he had loaded the mare with a dozen yards of stout homespun cloth, five pounds of maple sugar, a bearclaw necklace, a side of bacon and a beautifully tanned deerskin.

It was a trade he made, one of those sunny May mornings, that changed the whole direction of his journey. He came down into a narrow valley where a gristmill stood by the falls of a little creek. Because he needed corn meal he tied Martha to a tree and went over to the mill door. The slowly turning stones roared pleasantly and the dust danced in the sunlight. Bill waited until the miller pulled the wooden lever that turned off the power and let the water-wheel run free.

"Howdy, young feller," the man greeted his visitor. "Travelin' through?"

"Yes," said Bill, "I'm a Yankee peddler with a trunkful o' notions. I'm about out o' meal, and I wondered if you had any to sell."

"I'll measure some out fer ye right now. An' ye might take yer pack to the house. My woman's got a hankerin' fer doodads."

In a few moments the miller's wife was bending with clasped hands over the open trunk. "If only," she sighed, "we had enough money to git that there piece o' green silk! I could fix up my ol' black dress fer church-goin'."

Her husband looked uncomfortable. "How much would ye want fer it?" he asked Bill.

"There's a yard an' a half in the piece," the boy figured. "At three dollars that's four dollars an' a half."

The miller shook his head. "I don't see that much cash in a year," he said. "But say—mebbe we could figger out a swap, at that. Wait a bit."

He hurried out and Bill heard him climbing a ladder into the loft. When he returned he was carrying a queer-looking furry thing shaped like a big platter. "It's a prime beaver," he announced proudly. "Wuth four dollars in silver any place ye want to sell it."

Bill felt of the soft brown fur. He knew the man's estimate was conservative, and the piece of silk was a remnant he had bought for a dollar and a quarter. "It's a deal," he said, "if you want to throw in the corn meal. But tell me something. I thought all the beaver was trapped out o' this part o' the country. Where'd this one come from?"

"An old feller from south o' here, back in the woods, brung it in a couple o' months ago, an' traded me fer a sack o' meal. There's still a few skins trapped up there every winter. I shouldn't wonder if a body'd run into some more if he was to foller the crick-trail south."

Bill got to thinking, while he was eating his lunch of cold corn-cake beside the millpond. He knew that cash would be hard to find in the back-country settlements. Prime beaver-skins, on the other hand, were as good as money—better than the greenback currency that never brought its face value. If he left the main road and headed south through the hills he might be able to do some trading. And if he found there was no fur to be had he could always pick up a trail westward into the more settled farming regions.

It would be a hard journey, cut off from civilized comforts, but he had been roughing it long enough to have no fears about being able to take care of himself. He went back to the mill, asked the miller a few more questions and led the unprotesting mare up a narrow side trail into the woods.

The track he followed had never known a wheel. It was barely wide enough for Martha and her pack, and in places the twigs drummed on the tin trunk as they passed. Jody raced on ahead, happy to be in the forest.

Once that afternoon they saw a doe and her spotted fawn drifting like silent shadows across an opening in the woods. And when dusk fell and they made camp, the spring night was full of the rustling noises of small wild creatures. Bill lay awake a long time. He was quite comfortable in his blanket before the fire, but the thrill of being alone in a new country, miles from any dwelling place, kept his mind alert. The mare, Martha, was restless too. And Jody refused to lie down but roamed through the brush, his nose quivering at a hundred exciting scents.

It was the whistling snort of a buck, nosing at the ashes of the fire, that woke Bill just as the day dawned. He sat up and chuckled at the headlong rush the frightened deer made in departing.

That was the kind of country they moved through all day long. It was as wild as if no white man had ever passed that way. The woods were full of singing birds, and game of every sort was plentiful. If Bill had had any firearms with him, he might have dined on fresh meat instead of the smoked bacon that served as his main staple of diet.

The trail they were on followed the windings of the creek along a narrow valley that pushed upward into the hills. Sometimes it forded the stream or drove straight through the woods to avoid a roundabout bend. It was on one of these short-cuts that Jody suddenly put his nose to the ground and began to bay. Before the boy could stop him he had dashed away into the brush.

Bill was puzzled, for he had never heard the young dog give tongue like this before. Tracks of deer, rabbit and fox had all been passed over with scant attention, and he had begun to think Jody was completely worthless as a hunting dog. Now, however, the quavering voice came echoing back to him—the unmistakable cry of a hound on a hot trail.

After a moment the dog's bay changed to a sharp, excited yelping. Hurrying forward toward the sound, Bill wished that he carried a gun. He wished it all the more an instant later, when a bend in the trail brought him close enough to see what was happening.

Jody jumped around the foot of a huge dead oak tree barking with all his might. And in the hollow crotch, twenty feet above him, was the furry black bulk of a bear. The mare snorted, reared and jerked the halter out of Bill's hand. He did not run after her but stood where he was, looking up at the big beast in the tree. At first he thought the angry murmur that filled the air was the bear's growling. Then he saw a moving, circling cloud high among the trees, glinting in the sunlight like motes of bright dust. It was a swarm of wild bees, whose hive in the big oak the bear had been robbing.

Distracted by the valiant yapping of Jody, the animal left its tender nose unguarded for a moment. Bill heard a roar of pain as the bees darted in to sting. Then the bear deserted the high crotch and began scrambling hastily backward down the trunk.

"Jody!" the boy yelled. "Jody—come back!" But the little hound gave no sign of hearing him. Bill started forward at a run, his whole mind centered on snatching the dog out of danger. A sharp voice stopped him.

"Stay whar ye be!" Out of the brush stepped a lanky scarecrow of a man with a long-barreled rifle in his hands. He lifted the weapon without hurry, waited till the bear reached the ground and pulled the trigger. As the crashing report died away Bill saw the bear give a convulsive lurch, then topple in a heap. Jody dashed in, snapped at one outstretched paw and sprang away again.

The woodsman grinned at Bill. "Quite a b'ar dog ye got," he said. "Full o' gumption as all git out—or mebbe he jest don't know no better."

He was dressed in a greasy tow hunting shirt and buckskin leggings, and though the day was warm a cap of raccoon fur was pulled down over his long, matted, gray hair. The striped tail dangled behind to brush his shoulders. Still unhurried he strode forward to the dead bear, leaned his rifle carefully against a tree and whipped his long hunting-knife out of its sheath.

"Not sech a turrible good shot," he remarked critically. "I figgered on the eye but he swung his head. Thar's the hole, right back o' the eye. Good thing 'twa'n't no higher, or he'd ha' been full o' fight yit."

A few of the bees had followed their enemy down and still buzzed ominously around the dead bear. Bill slapped at one that came his way. "Aren't you afraid you'll get stung?" he asked.

"They don't trouble me," the woodsman chuckled. "Skin's too tough, I reckon. Glad to know whar that bee-tree is, though. Soon's they've got their new honey laid in I'll stop around this way myself."

"You live near by here?" Bill asked.

"Not fur. Jest up the crick. Whar you from?"

"I'm a peddler traveling through. My pack-horse ran off when she smelled the bear. I'd better go catch her."

He found old Martha with her halter tangled in the brush a hundred yards away. She was still nervous and trembly, but he talked to her soothingly and stroked her neck till she lost her fear. The skinning operation was well along when he returned. He led the mare a little way past the bee-tree and tied her to a sapling. Then he watched the woodsman rip the last of the hide off over the hind legs.

"I was sort o' lookin' for this feller," the man said. "He got one o' my hogs las' night, an' I been trackin' him. Not much fat on a b'ar this time o' year, but I might git a leetle good meat."

"What'll you do with the hide?"

" 'Tain't wuth carryin' to market—'specially a spring hide in poor fur. Reckon I'll make me another blanket out'n it. S'pose yore hoss'd stand fer packin' it, fur as my cabin? I'll tote the meat."

They rolled up the skin and loaded it across the fidgety mare's rump. Then the hunter led the way along the creek and up a side trail to a log shack in a tiny clearing. It was getting on in the afternoon and Bill accepted his invitation to have supper and spend the night.

The man's name, he learned, was Simon Baker, and he lived by himself. "Ain't many folks settled 'long here," he said. "That's why I like it. My pap brung me over from Pennsylvany when I was knee-high to a chipmunk."

His cabin was crude but comfortable. The puncheon floor was clean and the hearth was swept and tidy. As soon as he had a fire going, Baker greased the skillet and laid slabs of bear steak in it. A pleasant fragrance spread through the room as smoke rose from the sizzling meat.

Bill contributed enough corn meal and salt to mix a bannock and boiled water for tea. They sat together on a log outside the cabin and ate their supper. A pair of cardinals were whistling musically overhead, and after a moment one of them flashed past, a vivid spot against the green.

"Those red birds," Bill said. "I never saw one before till I got out this way. They're real pretty. What do you call 'em?"

"Jest redbirds is all, I reckon. Yeah, they're company fer a man."

Simon Baker took a home-made alderwood pipe out of his shirt and filled it with coarse black tobacco that he rolled with the heel of his hand. "Some o' my own leaf," he explained. "I grow me a leetle patch ever' year. Don't hev to depend on buyin' much. I got a private salt lick back in the woods. Even make my own clothes, sech as they be. Only thing I can't do is spin an' weave cloth."

"Maybe you could use some butternut homespun," Bill suggested cannily. "I picked up a few yards of it this side of Erie. Stout, solid stuff an' a good color for a hunting shirt."

When the woodsman expressed interest he went to his pack for the cloth. And within twenty minutes he had traded half the bolt, with two needles and a jew's-harp thrown in, for the four prime beaver-skins Baker had trapped that winter. Both of them were well satisfied with the bargain.

"Ye wouldn't want to swap that b'ar dog now, would ye?" the hunter asked. "Thar's some pups that's born to it, an' I reckon he's one."

Bill shook his head. "Jody's been through too

many scrapes with me," he said. "I wouldn't part with him now. Maybe you're right about his being a born bear-dog though. He's never wanted to hunt anything else, much."

The boy slept in the cabin that night, and at daybreak his host was up getting breakfast. Baker came out with him afterward to help lash the pack on the mare.

"Hmm," he remarked. "Expectin' her to foal pretty soon, ain't ye?"

Bill laughed. "Old Martha?" he asked. "I guess she's pretty old for anything like that."

"How old is she? Ever look at her teeth?"

Bill was ashamed to confess that he hadn't. They opened her mouth and examined the worn biting surfaces. "I make it sixteen," the woodsman announced. "What's yore reckonin'?"

"That's about it," Bill admitted. "Gosh! I wonder if you could be right, though. Funny I never thought of it."

Baker grinned. "Wal," he said, "my jedgment ain't no ways perfect. Still, I'd let her take it easy a couple o' days, if I was you."

CHAPTER

BILL adopted the old hunter's suggestion as he followed the creek-trail deeper into the wilderness. He was content to go slowly, and twice he stopped for an hour to let the .mare browse in the good grass by the stream. They came upon no more settlers that day. The

FOURTEEN

following morning however the boy sighted a big clearing ahead, with two cabins and several out-buildings. Dogs began barking at his approach and three or four youngsters, wild as young quail, scuttled to hiding-places behind the nearest log-house. Bill picked Jody up to keep him out of trouble and advanced till he was within hailing distance.

A lean, yellow-faced woman in a tattered deer-skin wrapper came to the door at his call. She had never seen a peddler before and answered vaguely when he asked if she wanted to trade for any of his goods. After a moment she began to tremble violently and retired into the shack.

"Maw's got the shakes," one of the less timid children explained. "Her fever 'n' ager gits her, 'bout this time ever' day."

"Where's your father?" Bill asked, and after a few moments one of the brood located him lying in the sun back of the barn. He came on unsteady legs, clawing the straw out of his beard.

"Jest finished my chill," he apologized. "Ain't no use fightin' the ager. Hev to give up fer an hour, that's all."

He shook his head when the boy offered to open his pack. "No money to buy nothin'," he said. "We're even short o' rations, tryin' to pull through till crop-time. I hed a litter o' pigs but the ol' sow took sick an' they died. All we got to live on now is corn meal."

Bill went to his pack and took out the side of bacon and the maple sugar. "This'll help a little," he said. "I don't know whether you've got anything to trade me, but I want you to have it anyhow."

"That's mighty kind," said the settler. "Couldn't take it 'thout a fair swap, though. I did trap a leetle fur las' winter—mebbe ye'd trade fer a couple o' beaver?"

He hurried to the house and produced two round birch stretchers with the skins sewn into them. They were not as fine as the fur Baker had caught but good enough.

"Guess 'twas sort of a Providence—yore comin' through this way," the grateful man told Bill. "We're too much off the main track to see many folks back here an' I'm tied down so I can't git out. It's a day's journey south to the road an' another half day to the store at Warren."

"Where's the road lead to, heading west?" Bill asked.

"Dunno's I ever heerd. Canton, mebbe—or St. Louis. Some one o' them places."

This information struck Bill as being a little

vague, but he thanked the settler and went on his way. A few rods along the trail he found himself wading through a swamp that stretched away on both sides of the creek channel. He thought he understood now why the family he had just left suffered from the ague.

In the afternoon the trail meandered upward over higher ground, rough with undergrowth and broken ledges. It was marked only with old blazes on the trees, and had been so little used that Bill had to stop often to throw fallen limbs out of the path. Old Martha moved at an even slower pace than usual, planting each hoof with care. She looked tired, hanging her head and panting whenever they stopped. Bill began to worry about her. Instead of pushing on till dusk he picked a camping place by the first small stream they reached and threw up a lean-to of dead poles. The sky was overcast, threatening rain. He worked as long as there was daylight, building a second lean-to for Martha and thatching them both with boughs. Then he made a fire and cooked his supper.

From the brook bank he gathered an armful of wild grass and put it within reach of the mare under her shelter. She munched a few mouthfuls of it but did not seem hungry. After a little she lay down quietly and Bill went back to his own bed.

It rained in the night, a gentle, soothing patter on the branches overhead. Jody whined and cuddled closer to his master. Then they both went to sleep. It was drizzling when day broke but the boy had kept fairly dry beneath his pole roof. Luckily he had taken the precaution to put some dead wood under the shelter the night before. After a few tries he started a fire and got breakfast.

When he went to see the mare she was still lying down. She looked up at him with patient eyes but in spite of his urging she made no effort to get to her feet. Troubled, Bill went back to his own shelter. For a while he occupied himself with checking over the goods in his pack. About half the stock in the tin trunk had been sold, and he rearranged its contents, packing in what was left of the bolt of homespun. His venture was not making him rich but he figured that with the beaver-skins he was at least breaking even.

Toward the middle of the morning he grew

restless and went off with the hound, exploring the course of the stream to the westward. They were gone two or three hours. On his return to the camp the first thing Bill did was to visit the sick mare.

He came to the front of the shelter and stopped, staring, a catch in his throat. Old Martha was on her feet. She looked gaunt and shaky in the knees, and her head was down, nuzzling at something half buried in the leaves. Bill had to look twice before he was sure. Then his face broke into a delighted grin. "Well, by jiminy crickets!" he whispered. "You really did it, old lady!"

The small brown bundle lying at her feet was a foal, its funny little head lifted and ears alert. Obeying the baby instinct of its kind it lay motionless, as if aware that some creature other than its mother was near.

Jody sniffed around outside the shelter but knew better than to come close. From a respectful distance he watched the new member of the family and wagged his tail in approval.

Bill spent the afternoon bringing grass to the mare and peeking discreetly into the lean-to to see how mother and child were getting on. Martha paid no attention to the fodder at first, but toward evening she showed signs of a returning appetite. The boy took some of his precious store of corn meal and salt and sprinkled them on the green hay as a special treat. After his own supper he carried water for the mare, making several trips with the cooking kettle before her thirst was quenched.

The rain had stopped next morning but continuing the journey was of course out of the question. Bill measured out what provisions he had left and put himself and Jody on short rations. He figured there was enough bacon and flour for three more meals, or four at the outside. There was no way of telling how long it might be before Martha and her baby would be strong enough to travel, so the food problem really worried him.

Several times that morning he considered leaving the mare and her foal and making a dash for the nearest settlement. But if the information given him by the man at the clearing was to be believed, he could not get back before late the next day. He thought of bears, still hungry after their winter sleep—of wildcats, whose shivery scream he had heard in the woods at night—and decided to stay where he could look after the helpless colt.

Meantime he set himself to find food near camp, if there was any to be had. Accompanied by the hound he went down to the edge of a bramble thicket and searched till he picked up a rabbit track. It was a barely perceptible trail that entered the tangle of briers just above the brook. Bill took some thin, strong twine from his pocket and looped it carefully. The free end he tied to a slender hickory shoot which he pulled downward, fastening the open noose across the entrance to the path. It was held in place there by a twig which the slightest pull on the loop would dislodge.

The crude snare was of a kind he had learned to set in New Hampshire, years before. He had small hope of catching anything, but it was the best he could do with the materials he owned. While he was tying the loop in the twine another idea came to him. There were half a dozen fish-hooks in his trunk—part of his stock of trade goods. He took all the string he had left, fastened one of the hooks to it, and cut himself an alder pole.

Ten minutes of industrious digging in the black earth by the bank produced three or four lively worms. With this equipment he set out down-

stream, looking for deeper water. On his trip of exploration the day before he had seen a pool that he thought might have fish in it.

When he came to it he was disappointed. The brook was almost narrow enough to jump across before it foamed over a ledge into the pool. Even there it was hardly more than five yards from bank to bank. Bill sat down on a log and baited his hook. First he tried floating the worm down from just below the fall. If there were fish in the dark water they gave no sign of interest. After a few minutes he weighted the line with a pebble and dropped the bait again in the deepest part of the pool.

He had barely had time to settle himself comfortably on the bank when he felt a lusty tug on his line. He raised the pole carefully lest he break the string, and played the fish up and down the pool for desperate minutes. At last he was able to pull his catch to the bank and lift it out, struggling and thrashing. It was a speckled trout that weighed well over a pound.

He fished for another hour and landed two more fish, smaller than the first but still big enough for the pan. Bill returned to camp well satisfied with his morning's work.

When he looked into the lean-to he laughed out loud with delight. The day-old foal was up on long, spraddly legs, its nose pressed eagerly under the mare's flank, its fuzzy little tail jerking with pleasure at the taste of the warm, sweet milk.

While the fire for the noon meal was making a bed of coals, Bill led the mare a few rods to a place on the brook-bank where she could both drink and find pasture of a sort. The colt went at her side, teetering awkwardly like a little boy on stilts. It was the first opportunity Bill had had for a good look at the new member of the clan. For lack of a better name he called him "Bub." It was short and it went with his diminutive size and his pert masculinity.

Bub's coat, now that it was dry, showed glints of gold in its bright chestnut color. He had a big white star in the middle of his forehead and his forelegs were white for several inches above the pasterns.

"By golly, Martha!" Bill exclaimed as he stared at the colt. "I don't blame you a mite for acting proud. He's a little beauty!"

Martha's pride expressed itself in unexpected ways. The boy had never thought of her as anything but meek and docile. Now she tossed her head saucily when he approached, stamped with an imperious forefoot, and even laid back her ears if he came too close to her precious infant.

Bill lunched well enough on fried trout and a small johnnycake. That afternoon he dug a hatful of dandelion greens and boiled them for his supper. The bitter, pungent mess would not have tempted him ordinarily, but after his long diet of corn and pork he had a craving for just this kind of food.

Early the following morning he found a good-sized cottontail rabbit fast in his snare, and before noon he caught two more fish. Thus provided, he knew he could feed himself and the dog for another day at least.

It was the third morning after the foal's arrival —the thirteenth day of May, as nearly as Bill could reckon—that he decided to move on. The rest had done Martha good. Her sides had filled out a little and her coat had grown sleeker. Even so, the boy hesitated to load her with the pack. He strapped it on his own shoulders and started off up the trail with the mare plodding cheerfully after him at the end of her lead-rope. The colt, who had already begun to learn the control of his legs, ambled close at her flank. And Jody ranged busily in front, behind or alongside the procession.

Every half hour or so Bill stopped to let the animals rest. Bub usually spent these moments in getting himself a little nourishment, while his mother browsed patiently on whatever grass she could find.

They made four or five miles by noon and then, after a longer rest, covered a similar distance before evening. Just as the sun set, Bill heard a horn echoing in the valley ahead. Through the trees he saw a ribbon of brown road and a four-horse coach pulling westward at a trot. He felt as if a load had been lifted from his shoulders. For here was the first wheeled vehicle, the first sign of civilized living that he had seen in a full week of wandering. He was content to camp where he was. Tomorrow he and his three dependents would be back in settled country.

CHAPTER

IT was noon of a fine warm May day when
Bill led his little procession up the dusty street
of Warren. The town slumbered in the sun,
its cross-roads store and tavern as quiet as if they
were deserted. In the fenced lot behind the tavern
a drove of hogs grunted lackadaisically and nosed

FIFTEEN

among the corn-shucks that had been thrown them
for fodder. Bill tied the mare to the hitching-rail
and went up the steps of the store.

Inside he found the proprietor asleep on a stool
tilted back against the counter. He tried rousing
him in an ordinary voice, then called more loudly.

When that had no effect he took a silver half dollar out of his pocket and let it fall on the counter.
At the ringing sound of the metal the storekeeper
woke so suddenly he almost fell off his stool.

"By gum!" he mumbled, rubbing his eyes.
"Wa'n't that cash money I heard?"

"Yes, sir," Bill grinned, and slipped the coin
back in his breeches. "But I reckon you'll be willing to trade for greenbacks, won't you?"

He bought a sack of corn meal and a slab of bacon, replenished his supply of tea, sugar and salt,
and asked about the roads. Warren was at the in-
tersection of two stage routes, one running south
from Ashtabula and the other coming over from
Pennsylvania and heading west to the towns on the
Ohio Canal. There was settled farming country
either way Bill might choose to go, and he finally
decided to continue his journey southward.

He ate a good dinner at the inn, treated the mare
to a feed of oats, and took to the road again in the
middle of the afternoon.

It was perhaps forty miles to New Lisbon, the
next town of any size. At the leisurely pace they
traveled, Bill allowed six days for the trip. The

little colt's legs were growing steadily stronger but the boy had no intention of injuring him.

It was a pleasant country they traveled through —long stretches of cleared land with the corn coming up in sturdy rows, young apple trees shedding white petals on the green grass, and cattle and sheep grazing everywhere. The farmers did not seem to have much money but they had plenty of everything else and welcomed the young peddler with a cordiality that made him feel completely at home. He sold a fair quantity of goods and took what he could get in trade. And meanwhile he ate at tables, slept in barns and talked politics like a civilized American.

Instead of the "movers" who thronged the westward highways, Bill encountered a more settled class of people along this road. Besides the stages and a few freight-wagons, the traffic was mostly made up of farmers on their way to mill or market, horse-traders and cattle drovers, and an occasional foot traveler like himself.

Not all these wayfarers were the sort of companions Bill would choose. The hard times had driven many disreputable characters to seek a living of sorts on the back-country roads. Some were merely unfortunates, too shiftless to work, who begged their way from farm to farm. Others were downright criminals who practiced horse-stealing and highway robbery when the opportunity offered. Even in this peaceful Ohio country most of the farmers kept loaded guns on the deerhorn racks above their fireplaces, and it was not uncommon for a stranger to find a big, savage dog chained to the doorstep, barring his way.

Bill got along well enough till he was a day's journey south of New Lisbon on the road to Cadiz. He had come to a stretch of woods that cloudy morning, and was tramping along through the shadows, wrapped in his own thoughts, when a voice hailed him. He looked around quickly and saw two men resting under the trees a few yards from the road. One of them had his back turned but the other, stretched out with his shoulders against a log, grinned and beckoned Bill to come closer. "What's yer hurry, Buddy?" he asked in a husky voice. "Got any vittles in that thar pack?"

The boy looked him over cautiously. He was a big fellow, fat around the midriff, but with none of the jollity of a fat man in his countenance. He wore nondescript clothing and battered cowhide boots, and his ragged beard was stained with tobacco juice. His companion, a smaller man, was sitting on a stump, scraping his cheeks with a razor. Bill noticed that his feet were clad in shapeless old slippers—odd footwear for the road. He did not look around but the boy caught the glint of his eyes reflected in the bit of mirror he was using, propped in the crotch of a tree.

"No," the young peddler answered. "I've only got what vittles I can use."

"Wal," the bearded man spat lazily, "no call to get huffy about it. Yankee, eh? Peddlin' notions?"

Bill nodded, clucked to the mare and went on without further parley. He didn't like the appearance of the strangers, and had no wish for their company.

That noon he cooked his lunch in the woods, off the road, and gave the animals their usual rest. When he returned to the highway he saw a man and woman tramping along some distance ahead of him. The man carried a big cloth bundle slung on a pole over his shoulder and they went slowly, as if they had walked a long way.

They went out of sight beyond a rise in the ground and Bill thought no more about them until he came to the next farmhouse, a mile or so beyond. As he approached the gate in the snake-fence and prepared to enter, he saw the couple just coming out.

The woman walked first, leading the man behind her by the hand. Bill realized then that her companion was blind. There were black patches over his eyes and he moved his big, unwieldy body hesitantly as if feeling for each step. He was clean-shaven and his mouth, drawn down at the corners, had a sullen, discontented look. He might have been any age from thirty to sixty.

The woman tugged her sightless comrade along as if she felt some need of hurry. She was clutching a paper parcel of food, evidently begged at the farmhouse, and her face was hidden in the tunnel of her faded sunbonnet. Something about the two figures, as they shuffled away down the road, made Bill stop and stare. Then he looked at the woman's feet. He was positive that those clumsy slippers showing below her dirty wrapper were the same pair he had seen on the smaller man back there in the woods.

Bill watched them for a moment before he turned in at the gate. A tall, shock-headed farm boy standing by the door gave him a civil greeting, and the woman of the house invited him in to show his wares.

"I reckon it's a lucky thing you happened to be at home," Bill told the boy. "That couple I just saw leaving here aren't up to any good." He described the two men he had encountered along the road. "The big one's no more blind than you are," he concluded. "An' the chances are they might have made trouble if they'd seen no men-folks around."

The housewife snorted and set her muscular arms akimbo. "The low-down trash!" she exclaimed. "Dressin' up thataway an' beggin' from honest folks! But they wouldn't've got far with me, I can tell you. That gun by the door's loaded, an' I know how to use it. Woman, indeed! I thought that was a mighty funny voice fer a decent woman to have!"

When her ire had subsided a little, she began to take some interest in the contents of Bill's trunk.

At the end of an hour he had sold her a comb, two or three pieces of ribbon and some lace edging, for which he received something over a dollar in cash. It was a good afternoon's work. He thanked her for her invitation to supper but explained that with several hours of daylight remaining he thought he had better push on.

Just after sunset, two or three miles farther along the road, he came to another stretch of woodland. "If there's water in that next hollow," he told Martha comfortingly, "we'll make camp right here, old lady."

As he had hoped, a few more steps brought them in sight of a shallow ford, and the wise mare quickened her pace in anticipation. At that moment Bill heard a twig snap in the roadside brush behind him. He turned quickly. Two men had come out of the woods—the same pair of scoundrels he had met before. The black patches were gone from the big man's eyes and in spite of his bulk he moved with a cat-footed tread. The other fellow had taken off his woman's dress. Bill was startled by the menace in his mean, small face.

"You git the hosses," growled the larger man.

"I'll take keer o' this young rooster."

Bill had no time to set himself for defense. Cumbered as he was with the pack, he could not have run away, if he had wanted to. But as his bulky antagonist leaped at him he swung a hard right with all his force. It landed squarely on the man's fat cheek and threw him off balance. And at the same instant Jody charged in, snarling and snapping at his legs. If Bill could have followed up that momentary advantage he might have knocked his assailant out. As it was he found the fellow's powerful arms grappling at his waist before he was able to launch another blow. A deft foot slipped behind his own and he was tripped, falling heavily on his side. The tin trunk hampered his struggles. In a few seconds his wrists and ankles were securely bound and the big ruffian, panting and cursing, was dragging him in among the trees.

There was a camp-fire blazing there and a kettle hanging over it. The clothes the pair had worn in their masquerade were tumbled in a heap near by. And tied by the hind leg to a sapling was a young pig, voicing its discomfort in plaintive squeals.

"You better git that shoat butchered," grumbled the big man. "He makes a sight too much racket."

"I ain't aimin' to give you first crack at the stuff in the pack," the other answered sullenly. "Open her up. Let's see what we got."

They tethered the mare to a tree and knelt together beside Bill's belongings. He rolled over so that he could watch them at their work, his heart sore with helpless rage. Jody, limping from the kicks he had received, crawled up to his master and tried to lick his face.

"Hm!" Bill heard the smaller man say. "Look at them beaver pelts! Five—six—seven of 'em."

"Ain't much else wuth anythin' here," his companion answered. "Lot o' women's gewgaws. Mebbe you could use 'em to dress up in, but I don't want 'em. Let's see if he's got any money."

The little man stood up suddenly. "Listen!" he whispered. "Hosses comin'. Stick a gag in the boy's mouth, quick. I'll shut that pig up."

Bill saw him snatch up an ax and silence the poor porker forever with a clout on the head. Then a piece of his trade calico was stuffed hastily into his own mouth. He could hear the thud of hoofs on the road now. Two horses, he thought, coming southward at a gallop. The big man tipped the kettle into the fire, quenching the flames in a hiss of steam, and everything was shadowy and quiet in the woods.

The riders, whoever they might be, were almost abreast of them now. Bill tried to cry out, but he could force no sound through the muffling folds of cloth. Then his heart leaped, for old Martha was neighing. Loud and clear her whinny rang out to greet the passing horses. He heard a man's voice. "Whoa!" it said, as the hoofs clattered to a halt. "Who's in thar?"

"Might be that young peddler feller," another voice answered. "We could ask if he's seen 'em."

They rode in through the deepening dusk and Bill recognized one of them as the shock-headed farmer boy. The other rider was tall and bearded. Both of them carried guns across their saddle-bows.

"Stay whar ye be," ordered the bearded man. "Drop that ax an' put yer hands over yer heads—higher. That's right. Now both of ye stand mighty still if ye want to keep on livin'. Fred, untie that lad an' let's see what's goin' on here."

In a moment the gag was pulled out of Bill's mouth and he drew a deep, grateful breath. While the boy loosened the ropes that bound his hands and feet he told his story. "If it hadn't been for that mare o' mine I guess I'd have been in a bad fix," he grinned. "They were just getting ready to divide up my goods between 'em."

"Gosh! They sure had ye trussed up," the other lad replied. "An' look what the skunks done to that shoat of ourn! Me an' Paw missed him out o' the hog-lot, an' I done figgered it might be them that had took him."

"All right, you boys!" the farmer called. "Take the ropes an' tie their hands in back of 'em. Don't be skeered o' gittin' 'em too tight, neither. I'll take 'em up to New Lisbon to the sheriff in the mornin'. Bring the pig along, Fred. We'll want it fer evidence."

He turned to Bill. "You all right, young feller?" he asked. "Be glad to have ye sleep with us if ye'd like."

Bill thanked him. "I wouldn't want to walk the colt back that far tonight," he said. "Guess I'll make camp right here. It doesn't look as if I'd be bothered by those two, at any rate."

The farmer laughed grimly. "Nope," said he. "They're goin' to be locked up in my root cellar fer the night."

Young Fred waved good-by and mounted his horse. With the two prisoners walking ahead, he and his father rode away northward. Bill, left alone in the grove, had time to appreciate his luck. "Whew!" he breathed. "That was a mighty close one, Jody. Let's see—did they hurt you?"

He built up the fire, started supper cooking and put his trade goods back into the pack. Before he turned in he gave the mare an armful of the tenderest clover he could find. "Without you, old gal," he told her, "I reckon this expedition would ha' been plumb on the rocks!"

CHAPTER

ALONG the road to Cadiz the days were warm with the approach of summer. Bill went at a leisurely pace. He was in no particular hurry to get anywhere, and he liked to give Martha plenty of time to feed on the good grass by the roadside. She was stronger and showed

SIXTEEN

more spirit than at any time since he first saw her, back in Vermont. And her condition was reflected in the thriving growth of the colt. Every day his little round barrel and buttocks looked plumper and he kicked his impudent heels higher.

While the mare grazed and Bub rested or played,

Bill would lie on his stomach and eat his fill of the wild strawberries that grew everywhere in the grass. Or he would turn over on his back and shade his eyes from the sun while he stared up at white clouds like the bellying sails of full-rigged ships, cruising across the blue. Such times he was almost too contented. It bothered his New England conscience to feel so lazy. After half an hour of daydreaming he was on his feet, eager to be on the road.

The mare carried the pack now, and Bill could swing along in freedom, sleeves rolled up and shirt open at the neck. He was burned as brown as an Indian by the sun.

As he worked south there were scattered settlements of thrifty German farmers, most of them from the Pennsylvania Dutch country. Their homesteads were kept neat as pins, with bright-colored flower-beds in every dooryard. He found them not much given to trading, but he was always sure of good food. Their tables groaned under the weight of those meals. Bill tasted strange dishes with stranger names—pig's knuckles and kraut—bauernwurst—wienerschnitzel. Often he was faced with five kinds of vegetables, three or four varieties of pickles and relishes, half a dozen preserves and two kinds of bread.

It was at one of these German farmhouses that he met a pair of fellow-travelers who journeyed with him for several days. They were a gray-haired, round-shouldered little fiddler named Fritz Kintner, and his daughter Greta. The gentle-faced musician was making his way afoot to the home of a son in Cincinnati. He had tramped all the way from New York, earning a few pennies for board and lodging by his playing. The girl took care of him like a mother. She was only sixteen, blue-eyed and red-cheeked, with long, straw-colored pigtails. She helped the farmers' wives with their baking, cleaning and soap-making, looked after their babies and made herself so useful that she and her father were welcome guests along the road.

The pair came to the door of a house where Bill had stopped to show his wares, one evening about dusk. The old man was limping wearily and his daughter held him half-supported on her strong young shoulder. She spoke to the housewife in German—a language of which Bill had picked up only a few words.

The wayfarers were invited in at once and supper was set out for them. As soon as the meal was over and the dishes done, the old musician opened his violin case to play. Bill had been helping the farmer with the chores for the privilege of sleeping in the barn. At the first strains of music, the German dropped his pitch-fork and listened. "Come!" he whispered. "Ve go in now. Dot moosic! Ach—it's beaudiful!"

They took off their dirty boots by the step and tiptoed into the house. The old man was sitting on a home-made kitchen chair, the fiddle tucked under his chin, his eyes fixed dreamily on something far away. He played simple little German folk-songs that brought sentimental tears to the eyes of the good farm people. After a while Greta began to sing, in a clear, true voice and soon the household joined her, beating the time with their feet, shouting the choruses and laughing with joy.

Bill stayed for an hour, and when he and Jody crept into the hay in the big, dark barn, he could still hear the notes of the violin coming sweetly through the summer night.

At the town of Cadiz the road from Pittsburgh and Steubenville joined the one Bill had been following and the wagons of emigrants appeared once more. There were fewer of them now and they were hurrying to reach their new homes in time to plant some kind of crops. Already it was well into June, and the corn was tall in the fields they passed. So there was a great prodding of oxen and lashing of tired horses.

Fritz Kintner and his daughter tramped along with Bill on the way to Cambridge. The fiddle-case and their little bundle of belongings were added to Martha's load, and the old musician seemed to regain some of his strength when he had nothing to carry.

It was pleasant having company on the road. Bill heard many tales about the old country and its customs, and he in turn tried to describe the life in his own New Hampshire hills. The old man shivered at his description of the long, snowbound winters. It had been bad enough in New York, he said. He hoped that Cincinnati would have a warmer climate.

Sometimes they all stopped together when Bill

went to a farmhouse to peddle his goods. More often the man and the girl went on ahead at their slower pace, and Bill caught up with them an hour or two later. Greta's cooking was an agreeable change after a long succession of bachelor meals. The corn and bacon from Bill's pack seemed to take on a new flavor when she prepared them.

The boy was sorry to part with his friends at Cambridge, but they were heading west on the National Road to Zanesville, and he had decided to continue southward by less-traveled highways. He had found it harder to sell his notions in places where there were stores. If he was to dispose of the merchandise that still remained in his trunk he knew he would have to find a region of good farms that lay off the beaten track.

It was haying time when he reached Cambridge. A few miles south of the town Bill came to a big bottom-land farm where two mowers were busy cutting timothy in a field close to the road. As he started up the lane towards the house, the farmer hailed him.

"You look strong, young feller," he said. "Ever swing a scythe?"

Bill replied modestly that he didn't think he was bad at it.

"If ye ain't in a rush to git somewhere," the farmer told him, "we could use a stout hayin' hand. Let's see ye work a bit. If ye take hold smart I'll pay a dollar a day an' found."

The boy tied the mare to the snake-fence and climbed over. "Let's have the scythe," he answered.

He whetted the blade, gripped the handles and swung rhythmically into the swath the farmer had left. Mowing was a job he liked. The other man was already fifty yards ahead, but by the time they had made a circuit of the field, Bill was right on his heels.

"Reckon ye're hired," the farmer grinned. "I'll take yer mare up to the barn. Say—that's a mighty pretty colt! Don't aim to sell him, do ye?"

Bill laughed. "I want to keep him long enough to see what kind of a horse he makes, if I can. He might turn out to be fast, you know."

"Mm," the farmer nodded. "Jest what I was thinkin'. Well, you fellers keep at it. I'd like to git this field in the barn 'fore tomorrer night if the weather holds. Come up to dinner when ye hear the horn."

Bill stayed there for three weeks. He worked hard from early morning till dark, sweated and toughened under the broiling sun, blistered his palms on the handles of scythe, rake and fork, and saw the blisters turn to thick, horny calluses. Meanwhile he ate his fill of good, plain food and slept like a log every night. When he left he had eighteen dollars to add to his little store of greenbacks and silver.

"Where ye headin' fer now?" the farmer asked him as he tied the pack on Martha's back.

"I'll keep on south, I guess, till I hit the Muskingum," Bill replied. "I've still got a few dollars' worth of stuff here to sell."

" 'Tain't a bad country," his employer nodded. "Ye'll run into Quakers down there. Pennsylvany folks. Some says they're almighty close traders, but I've allus got on with 'em. They talk sort o' queer —all 'thee's' an' 'thy's'—an' there ain't a mite o' doubt about their bein' thrifty. But they're square an' peaceful. Make good neighbors. I wouldn't count on sellin' many gewgaws to the women, 'cause they dress pretty plain. Ye'll find they've got cash fer anything they need, though. There's jest one thing more." He hesitated. "Some folks think the Quakers is abolitioners. There's talk about their helpin' runaway slaves through to Canady. I dunno what yer politics is, but I'm jest tellin' ye, so ye'll be warned."

Bill hadn't given much thought to the slavery question. Like most New Englanders he regarded slave-holding as wrong in principle, but it was a long way off and no particular business of his. On his way southward he had seen colored people in increasing numbers—free Negroes who had little farms or hired out for days' work. He had grown used to their funny, slurring talk and the mellow huskiness of their voices. They were folks, not so very different from white folks, and it seemed a strange thing that only eighty miles away, across the Ohio River, they were bought and sold, owned and driven like cattle. Still, it was the law of the land and nothing for him to worry about. He said good-by to the farmer and set off in high spirits.

For the next few days Bill devoted himself to peddling rather than to traveling. He went only a few miles each day, but by stopping at every farmhouse he steadily reduced his stock of notions. With hay under shingles and the other crops shaping up well, nearly everybody along the road was in a buying mood.

On the fifteenth of July the boy checked over the goods left in his trunk. A few yards of plain calico, three or four knives, a pair of scissors and a string of colored beads made up the total. There were also the necklace of bear-claws and the doeskin, but those he thought he would not sell. Bill sat on a log in the sun by the roadside and did some thinking. He could turn back now and be sure of disposing of what he had on hand before retracing many miles. But he liked this country. He was having an adventure that he might never be able to repeat. There was nothing to take him home—no prospect except a possible job in the mill—and the full tide of summer called him southward. There were fat ears of sweet corn on the tall stalks now, and peaches were ripening fast in the orchards. Just by reaching behind him he could pick a whole handful of the big, juicy blackberries that grew wild along the fence.

"Shucks!" he grinned. "Who wants to go back

now? What do you say, Jody—Martha? Let's keep on a ways. We might even get as far's the Ohio River!"

So they plodded on through the morning, rested in a shady grove during the noonday heat, and resumed their journey in the cool of the afternoon. It was about five o'clock when Bill sighted a horseman riding up the narrow road toward them. There was nothing out of the ordinary in such a meeting. But something about this particular horse and rider riveted the boy's attention. He thought he had never seen a lovelier saddle animal. It was a slim, high-headed black, with fine, clean legs and dainty hoofs. Sitting easily erect in the saddle, the rider was as unusual as his mount. A broad-brimmed, low-crowned gray hat was tilted rakishly on his dark curls, and he wore an elegant gray cloak thrown back from his shoulders. Tight-fitting fawn breeches and expensive riding boots encased his slender legs. His face, shadowed by the brim of the hat, was pale but strikingly handsome in an arrogant way. As he rode closer his dark, sleepy-looking eyes flicked over Bill like the touch of a whip.

He reined the blooded black horse across the boy's path and looked down at him with what might have been meant for a smile.

"I'm makin' inquiries, young man," he said softly. "In the co'se o' yo' travels have you chanced across any nigras that you thought might be runnin' away?"

Bill stared at him. "No," he said. "What would they look like?"

The horse pawed and pranced and the rider curbed him with a firm hand. "My man Cletus an' a boy about twelve answerin' to the name o' Banjo," he replied. "The man's six foot an' over—a prime field-hand but sulky. Chain scars on his laigs, an' one ear cropped with a 'V.' No marks on the boy —yet."

He hesitated a moment or two as if considering. "There might be a reward fo' the one that repo'ted 'em," he added, looking at Bill's ragged clothes. "Twenty-five dollars on each of 'em. An' o' co'se you're aware o' what the law says about helpin' a slave to escape? The penalty, in case yo' memory is faulty, is five hundred dollars fine or jail."

He nodded carelessly, gave rein to the restive

black and danced away northward.

Bill stood looking after them till horse and rider had vanished around the next bend. From the man's speech and dress and the fine horse he rode, he must be a planter from one of the Southern States. Kentucky, perhaps, or Virginia. A smooth-talking customer, but under his courtly manner he was hard, Bill thought—hard as steel. The boy wondered if there had been pistols beneath the saddle flaps.

A mile or two farther on he came in sight of a little hamlet where two roads crossed. Half a dozen houses clustered in the shade of maples on a long, low hill. Hot and tired, the boy led his dusty little caravan into the shadow of the trees and stopped by a hollowed half-log that served as a watering-trough. A wooden pipe led to it from a spring in the side of the hill and a constant trickle of clear, cold water kept it filled.

The beasts drank gratefully while Bill caught a dipperful of the sparkling water from the spout. When his thirst was quenched he looked around him to see where he might be. One of the houses was a plain, small, white-painted frame building with two doors and a long, open horse-shed in the rear. He took it for a school-house until he noticed the small sign that stood by the roadside. "Sugar Ridge Friends' Meeting" was the inscription painted on it.

A few yards beyond Bill saw two old men sitting under a tree, enjoying the cool of the late afternoon. They had not noticed his approach. From their voices he judged that one of them must be hard of hearing.

"Mebbe it's right in the eyes o' the Lord," one graybeard was shouting, "but I still say it's a pesky dangerous thing to fool with. Tobias is a keerful man but he's bound to git hisself in trouble sooner or later."

The other man nodded. "That Virginny feller means business, too," he said. "Did ye take note o' the hoss he was ridin'? Ain't many like that this side o' the river, I reckon. A real thoroughbred!"

Bill would gladly have heard more but at that moment one of the ancients caught sight of him and nudged his companion. Their conversation ceased at once and they sat staring owlishly as the little pack-train approached. The boy nodded a good evening and tramped on down the road.

That night he camped in a piece of woods that bordered a peach-orchard. In the dusk, after supper, he made his way among the heavily laden trees and picked several of the biggest and ripest peaches for his dessert. Their flavor was a rare treat to his New Hampshire palate. He had never tasted peaches but once or twice before in his life.

Bill had been asleep for several hours when he was roused by Jody's growling. The night was pitch-black and the air heavy with threatening storm. Along the southern horizon faint glimmers of heat-lightning played fitfully. Bill sat up, holding his breath as he listened. Not a sound broke the stillness except the whispered rumble in the hound's throat. The boy was about to lie down again when a twig snapped a little way off in the woods and Jody shook with a spasm of yelping barks.

The crackling in the underbrush came again, farther away, and then Bill heard another sound— the pounding slap of feet on the road. Somebody was running, and running fast.

CHAPTER

THE thunderstorm must have rolled off up the Muskingum Valley, for Bill woke next morning to find the ground dry and the sky clear. He whistled blithely as he went about his breakfast-getting. The noise he had heard in the night was almost forgotten till he saw Jody nosing

236

SEVENTEEN

industriously among the saplings a few yards from
the camp-fire. Then his curiosity was aroused. He
followed the dog through broken underbrush for
some distance till they came to the road. And there
in the dust at the edge of the weeds he saw a man's
track. Big—barefooted—splay-toed. In an instant

a picture came to his mind. "Six foot and over . . . chain scars on his legs . . . one ear cropped with a 'V.' " Bill shivered as he thought of the terror the hunted Negro must have felt when Jody began to bark. But though he looked up and down the roadside for several minutes, he found no trace of the smaller footprint he sought—the track of the boy called "Banjo."

It was another hot day. Bill went slowly and let the mare graze along the way. Twice he stopped at big, well-kept farmhouses, hoping to make some sales. But the prim Quaker ladies who greeted him with such gentle politeness were not to be persuaded into buying. One of them looked a shade wistfully at the colorful glitter of the glass bead necklace before she turned away. "Thee sees," she explained, "we Friends are not much given to worldly dressing. I think I might be able to use that pair of scissors, though. And before thee goes I hope thee'll have a doughnut and a glass of cold buttermilk."

He made a long noonday stop in the shade of a grove of hickories. Late in the afternoon he passed a long, rolling field where four or five men were at work harvesting oats. Beyond the golden stubble he saw a huge red barn and a comfortable-looking white house, set back from the road and half hidden by shade trees. Lettered neatly on the broad gate post was a name—"TOBIAS HALSEY."

Bill debated with himself whether to go in or to keep on as long as the daylight lasted. There was a hospitable charm about the place that made him want to stop. It was Jody who decided him. The little hound sniffed at the trampled earth a moment and went trotting up the lane toward the house as if he lived there.

Long before Bill reached the honeysuckle-covered porch he heard sounds coming from inside—a chatter of female voices that would have terrified him if it had not sounded so contagiously good-natured. He tied the mare to the hitching-post and had lifted his hand to knock at the door when it suddenly flew open. He had a momentary vision of an eager face and bobbing red-gold pigtails. Then there was a swish of skirts and the girl vanished. "Oh, Mother!" he heard her cry. "Come quick! It's a peddler!"

"Very well," a placid voice answered from the kitchen. "Why doesn't thee ask him in, Phoebe?"

At that the mischievous face reappeared and Bill saw a finger beckoning.

"Shall I bring my pack?" he asked.

"Oh, yes—of course!" replied Phoebe. "Bring it right out back. Mother's busy paring peaches."

Following his young guide, Bill carried the tin trunk through the house. At the kitchen door he stopped, flustered by what he saw. It was a big room but it seemed to be overflowing with domestic activity. By the long deal table sat a big, motherly woman in a blue apron, her short-bladed knife flying swiftly above a basket of rosy-cheeked peaches. Between the table and the steaming kettles on the cookstove two grown girls bustled about. Their hair was the same ruddy shade as Phoebe's, but they wore it in demure knots instead of flying braids. And stalking about among the busy feet was an immense tortoise-shell cat.

"Come right in," the elderly woman nodded. "Thee'll find a place to open thy pack on the end of the table there."

Bill displayed such few wares as he had left while the three girls leaned closer with a chorus of "Oh's" and "Ah's."

"Mother!" he heard Phoebe whispering. "The beads! Wouldn't they go lovely with my new brown dress?"

Her mother smiled. "Can thee imagine what some of the plain Friends would say, if thee wore them to Meeting?" she said. "But I understand, little daughter. Yes, thee may get them if they don't cost too much." She looked at Bill inquiringly.

"It's my last string o' beads," he grinned, "so I'm willing to knock off a little. The regular price is half a dollar. Would forty cents be all right?"

"Thee has thy own money, Phoebe," said the gray-haired woman. "Does thee want to spend forty cents? Remember—that's more than thee gets for three dozen eggs."

Phoebe answered not a word but sped away joyfully to get her purse. Meanwhile the older girls fingered the calico and discussed their needs. In a few minutes the boy had sold everything in his trunk except two pocket-knives. And the mother quietly purchased one of those. "My boy Eben has a birthday next month," she explained. "I've been meaning to get a present for him and this is just the thing."

Bill laughed. "I guess this is the end o' my peddling trip," he remarked. "That other knife I'll
just keep for luck."

They asked him about his journey and listened
with lively interest as he told some of his adven-
tures. When the kitchen clock struck six he started
to shoulder his trunk.

"No, no," Mrs. Halsey told him firmly. "There's
plenty of room for thee and thy animals. The men-
folks'll be in from the fields in a minute. Sarah—
go ring the bell."

Bill saw the girl go to the pull-rope of a big brass
bell in the yard and give a lusty tug or two that set
it clanging. Soon he heard masculine voices and a
tramp of heavy feet. There was a scurrying of the
girls to finish setting the table and a mighty splashing at the pump. Then men and boys came troop-
ing into the kitchen.

Bill was introduced to the whole family before
they sat down at table. In addition to the girls,
Lucy, Sarah and Phoebe, whom he had already
met, there were Tobias Halsey and his four big
sons—Noah, Abijah, Moses and Ebenezer. The

youngest boy, called Eben for short, was about Bill's age—a husky youngster, broad-shouldered and red-haired like most of his brothers and sisters.

The whole big family bowed their heads in a silent grace, then attacked the mighty platters and serving dishes of food with healthy appetites. There were chicken and dumplings, tender corn on the cob, boiled new potatoes and green peas. And to top off the feast the girls brought on an immense biscuit shortcake overflowing with peaches and whipped cream.

When the meal was over the girls began clearing away the plates. The older boys had gone out to do the milking and only the parents, Eben and Bill were left at the table.

Mrs. Halsey glanced at her husband. "Our young friend has been telling us of happenings along the road, Tobias," she said. "A day's journey north he was stopped by a southern gentleman looking for slaves."

Tobias Halsey's expression did not change as he nodded. He was a big man, strongly built, with a weather-seamed face and a firm jaw. Bill thought he looked forbiddingly stern until he noticed the

humorous crinkles at the corners of the man's calm
blue eyes.

"That might be the man who stopped here," he
answered. "How would thee describe him, lad?"

"His clothes were mighty fine," said the boy.
"Gray hat and cloak. Light tan-colored breeches
and extra special boots. And he was riding the
grandest black horse I ever saw. He spoke of a reward for two runaway slaves—a man called Cletus
and a boy, Banjo."

The Quaker nodded again. "The same man,
right enough," he said. "A Virginian named Ransome Cawley. And had thee seen these colored
people?"

"No," Bill replied. "Not then, anyhow. Last
night I reckon I heard one of 'em, though." He
told about the noise in the brush and the track he
had found that morning.

Tobias Halsey listened attentively but made no
comment. "Eben," he told his son, as they rose
from the table, "thee can show our guest where to
stable his livestock." His eye twinkled at the word.
"The two of you can sleep in the loft tonight."

Eben grinned shyly and accompanied Bill into

the yard. "That's a mighty cute colt," he said admiringly. "He's awful young, isn't he?"

"Round about nine weeks," Bill answered. "He's real active, though. He's come a hundred an' fifty miles under his own power!"

They took the animals into the big barn, fragrant with new hay. The mows of clover and timothy reached upward in rustling mountains to the darkness under the roof. The mare and her foal were placed in an empty box-stall and Eben brought a measure of oats and a big forkful of hay. Jody meanwhile was sniffing busily around the barn floor.

"Must be rats he's after," the Quaker boy remarked. "The cats keep 'em down mostly, but around grain harvest they're always a nuisance."

Bill said nothing. He had seen the dog follow some kind of scent to the foot of a ladder leading upward along the face of the mow, and he knew of no rats that climbed ladders. At that moment a barely perceptible sound made him glance up quickly. High up in the wall of hay a round brown head appeared for an instant. He caught the flash of scared white eyeballs and then the face was gone.

Startled, Bill looked at Eben. The young Quaker flushed and a worried expression came into his eyes. For several seconds the two boys stared at each other, saying nothing. Finally Eben motioned to the New Englander to follow him. "Come on out back o' the barn where we can talk," he said in a low voice.

They sat down under a pear-tree between the chicken-run and the barn wall. Eben plucked a grass-stem and chewed on it thoughtfully. His face was serious.

"I'm going to tell thee the truth," he began. "Father says it don't pay to lie, even to protect a runaway. There'd have been no need to speak to thee about it at all if thee hadn't seen the boy just now."

He stood up and looked about carefully before he continued, his voice hardly above a whisper. "I don't know how thee feels about slavery, but with us it's a matter of conscience. When a colored man who wants to be free comes this way we help him, law or no law. This farm's a station on what they call the 'Underground Railroad.' In the last five years I reckon Father's helped nigh onto a hundred slaves on their way to Canada."

Bill was tingling with excitement. "I've heard o' the Underground," he said. "How do you manage, though, without getting caught?"

"Father did have to pay the fine once, a couple of years back," the other boy replied. "But he's mighty careful, and most of the folks 'round here feel the same way we do. I reckon they all know about it and just keep their mouths shut."

"How do the slaves know how to find you?" asked Bill.

"Somebody from the next station south generally brings 'em up here in the night. We don't always know they're coming, but we're ready any time to hide 'em or ship 'em on, whichever seems to be the best idea. Sometimes they ride clear to Cambridge in a load o' fodder we're taking to market. The slave-catchers are onto that, though. They'll stop any farmer's wagon and search it, these days. The last few weeks they've been coming up to the house, too, asking questions. That southerner thee saw—Ransome Cawley—stopped up here two days ago and seemed mighty suspicious. His slave Cletus was hid in the barn along with young Banjo, at the time, and must have heard him talking. Anyhow, instead of waiting for us to take him on like we promised, the darky cut and ran that night. It was probably him thee heard in the woods. No telling—he may have been caught by now, poor chap."

"Gosh!" Bill murmured. "I hope he got away. What do you figure to do with the boy?"

"I don't know," said Eben, "but Father's bound to find some way. He thinks out all kinds of plans."

Twilight was stealing up over the fields and the older boys had finished their evening chores. Bill heard them putting the milk to cool, down at the spring-house.

"Listen," Eben told him. "Thee'd better go in, and don't say anything about our talk. I've got to get some food in the kitchen and take it to Banjo."

Half an hour later, when the whole family was assembled in the candle-lit parlor, Tobias Halsey read a chapter from the Bible and good-nights were said. The two boys groped their way up a ladder to the loft over the woodshed. Open windows at front and rear allowed a cool draft of air to circulate through the low, raftered room. Bill slipped off his clothes and lay down beside Eben on the hard straw mattress of the double bed.

It seemed no time at all until the slow, even breathing of the Quaker boy told Bill he was asleep. For his own part he was wakeful. The gentle evening breeze, the friendly dark and the peaceful chirp of crickets should have made him drowsy, but he lay there for a long time thinking about the Underground Railroad and that fleeting glimpse he had caught of the frightened little colored boy in the haymow.

He was just drifting off at last, when a sound jerked him back to full consciousness. Coming up the lane toward the house he heard a soft thud of hoofs and a murmur of voices. Then Jody barked. Bill sat up, listening intently. He wondered whether he should wake his companion, but decided against it. He would feel pretty foolish if it turned out there was no significance in this late visit. Slipping noiselessly out of bed he tiptoed across to the front window and crouched there looking down into the dark dooryard.

CHAPTER

IN the dim starlight Bill could make out the shapes of two horses, one black, the other a lighter color—roan perhaps. It was impossible to see much of the riders. They had stopped talking now and rode at a walk into the deeper darkness under the trees.

EIGHTEEN

There was a sound of boots on the porch steps, followed by a sharp knock at the door. For a moment the house was quiet. Then the floor creaked and a flicker of yellow light shone on the leaves. Bill heard the door-latch lifted. The roof of the porch hid the doorway but he could hear every word that was spoken.

"Good evenin', Mr. Halsey, suh." It was a softly mocking southern voice that the boy had heard before. "Sorry to call a gentleman out o' bed, but there's valuable property concerned."

"I'll be glad to oblige thee if thee'll state thy business," the Quaker answered calmly.

"Well, suh, it's those two nigras o' mine," drawled the Virginian. "We've reason to believe they're hidin' somewhere around yo' place."

"I can tell thee plainly that no two Negroes of thine or anyone else's are on this farm," was Tobias Halsey's reply. "Does that satisfy thee?"

A shade of stiffness came into Cawley's voice. "I would hesitate to question yo' word, suh, but it may be that they're here without yo' knowledge. Mr. Weeden, will you come here, suh?"

In such faint light as the Quaker's candle gave, Bill saw the second rider dismount and move toward the steps. He was a short, stoutish man in a tail-coat and moth-eaten beaver hat.

"Tobias," he said querulously, "I sure hate to bother ye like this, but the gentleman seems to have pretty good evidence his niggers come this way. An' as deputy marshal I got to give him assistance in findin' 'em."

"What does thee propose to do, then?" asked the farmer evenly. "Does thee have a warrant to search the house?"

"Warrant? Well—no," the officer replied. "Thought ye wouldn't mind our lookin' around a bit, though."

"Jacob Weeden," said Halsey, "did thee ever know me to tell a lie?"

"Can't say as I did, Tobias."

"Then I tell thee now that no amount of looking around this property will find the pair of Negroes thy friend is after. If thee still wants to waste thy time, go ahead."

Bill heard a footstep behind him and in another moment Eben had joined him at the window. There was an uncomfortable silence outside. Then the deputy marshal's voice came up to them. "I tell ye, it ain't no use huntin', Mr. Cawley," he urged. "If he says they ain't here, they ain't, an' that's a fact."

"Jake's worried now," Eben whispered. "He knows anything Father says, he means."

The slave-owner stepped down from the porch, still polite. "I'll bid you good evenin', suh," he said. "Sorry we disturbed you. But I'll have to give you warnin' that I'll be watchin' this place mighty sharp."

He mounted lightly and swung the curvetting black toward the road, followed by the discomfited deputy. Behind them the candle-beam was cut off by the closing door.

"Come on," said Eben. "Put on some clothes an' let's go down. Father'll hold a council, I reckon."

In the kitchen they found Tobias Halsey and Abijah, half-dressed, standing by the table. Noah came a moment later and after him Moses. The farmer looked around at the faces of his sons. His glance halted when it came to Bill, but a nod from Eben answered his unspoken question and he pinched out the candle between a horny thumb and forefinger. In the dark his low voice sounded solemn.

"The boy Banjo has got to be sent on tonight or first thing in the morning," he said. "They'll be waiting for him up the line. I don't think it will be easy this time, for I judge Mr. Cawley is keeping watch, just as he promised."

There was a long silence. Finally one of the grown sons—Bill thought it was Noah—spoke slowly. "I'm willing to try it with a hayrack-load of oats," he began. "We've managed before, that way—and—"

"Not this time," his father stopped him. "Thee would run into trouble before thee'd gone a mile. It will need to be a better plan than that."

The silence was even longer when he finished. Bill shifted uneasily and drew a deep breath. "Maybe I could help," he said. "I reckon that deputy marshal would know any of you by sight. The other one has seen me but he hasn't any idea I've been here. How big is the colored boy?"

"Not very big," Eben answered. "He's about ten, I'd say, and small for his age. His folks are in Canada already and he's trying to get to 'em."

"Well, I've got a plan that might work," said Bill.

"Wait a bit," the Quaker put in kindly. "Is thee sure thee understands the risks in this business? It's a fine thing for thee to offer, but I'm not certain I should let thee undertake it."

Bill was in earnest. "I know what I'm up against," he answered soberly. "I've looked that slave-catcher in the eye an' I know he's bad—he'd shoot in a second if he was riled. But I wouldn't ever feel right if I didn't try it. Anyhow, let me tell you my idea. You can see what you think of it."

For ten minutes the whispered consulation went on. At the end Tobias Halsey groped in the dark and laid a hand on Bill's shoulder. "Thee's a brave lad, and a smart one," he said. "I'm going to trust thee. Plenty of time to get some sleep now, so off to bed, boys."

．　　．　　．　　．　　．　　．　　．

Breakfast, next morning, was a quieter occasion than supper had been. The girls' chatter was silenced. Bill caught Phoebe stealing a troubled glance at him across the hot biscuits and syrup. The older boys ate stolidly but no one else seemed to have much appetite. Bill thought of the old New England expression—"journey-proud"—and smiled in spite of the nervous feeling in his diaphragm.

When the meal was over they sat for a long minute with heads bowed. Bill felt better after that reverent stillness. It was as if some of the strength and steadiness of these friendly people had become part of him.

Tobias Halsey took him aside for a few final instructions. "Eben'll help thee load up," he said. "If they're watching it's better they shouldn't see me go out with thee. Banjo knows what to do. I'm confident thee'll get him through."

At the door Mrs. Halsey pressed a bundle into his hand. "It's some lunch I put up," she smiled. "Thee may not have much time for cooking, along the road."

Eben was waiting for him in the barn. "The mare's been fed and watered," he told him. "That sack of green corn's ready too, right in the stall with her. Think thee can handle it alone? Thee'll have to later, if everything goes well."

Bill examined the long, stout burlap bag that lay on the floor beside the mare. It was stuffed with ears of corn that rustled in their green sheaths and overflowed at the ends, where the sack was tied.

"Doesn't look so very heavy," Bill grinned. He clasped it around the middle and lifted it off the floor. With a heave he laid the awkward bundle across the mare's back, with the ends hanging down on either side. Leaning close, he addressed a low word or two to the bag. "Yassuh," came a whispered answer. "Ah'll ride fine."

"All right," said Bill. "Now don't say another word, no matter what happens. We'll get you tied on an' then we'll start."

Methodically Bill took his pack-line and threw a double hitch over the plump sack and the roll of duffel he had laid across Martha's withers. The lunch he placed in his empty trunk and slung it on his shoulders. Then with a quick grip of Eben's hand he took the lead-rope and marched out of the barn.

After a curious sniff or two at the bag of corn, Jody trotted ahead unconcernedly, while Bub pranced along at his mother's side. Bill looked up as he passed the house. Phoebe was there at the window, her nose pressed against the glass, and he waved to her gaily before starting down the lane.

The dew was still on the grass and the long shadows of early morning stretched westward from every tree and bush. Bill's watchful eyes scanned both sides of the road, but he walked along with a hearty stride and whistled as if he hadn't a care in the world. Half a mile north of the farm he approached a patch of woodland where two sad-dled horses—a black and a roan—stood tethered in the shade. At first he could see nothing of the men who owned them. But as he came nearer, Cawley and Weeden rose from behind a thicket and stepped out into the road.

The planter eyed him coldly, taking in every de-tail of his accouterments and the mare's pack. Bill felt a sudden chill of fear. Suppose something had slipped, or the end of the sack had come open! He had a desperate impulse to look back, but forced himself to keep his eyes on the men in front of him. Nodding a cheerful good morning he was about to pass when the Virginian held up a per-emptory hand.

"Wait a bit, my friend," he said. "There's a few questions I'd like to ask. Seems to me you were headin' south when I last met you."

Briefly Bill explained that he had sold the last of his goods and was going homeward—back to New Hampshire, he guessed. In answer to other queries he told them the bag on the mare's back contained sweet corn he had taken in trade; that he had been keeping watch along the road but had not seen any two darkies who looked as if they were runaways; that he would be glad to continue looking for them, because he sure could use that fifty dollars.

He shook in his boots when Cawley passed a casual hand over the surface of the sack and pulled a corn husk or two out of one end. But at length the pair seemed to be satisfied.

"The boy's a Yankee, fair enough," Weeden commented. "Anybody can tell by the way he talks. An' ye ain't hooked up with the Quakers, are ye, boy?"

Bill laughed. "Not me," he said. "I've seen some of 'em down this way. Tighter'n a drumhead. I didn't sell 'em a paper o' pins."

Not until he was a good hundred yards beyond did he dare to draw an easy breath. He could still feel a trembling in his knees, but he was so relieved to have passed the test of that encounter that he hummed a tune as he walked.

"Banjo," he said in a low voice, when they had reached an open place with no possible listeners—

"Banjo, you did fine back there. Can you breathe all right?"

"Yassuh," came a shaky whisper. "Ah's 'most skeert to deaf, but Ah kin breave. Is dey gone?"

"Yes," Bill answered shortly. "But they might come back. You just be quiet now, 'cause we've got a long way to go."

It was thirty miles from the Halsey farm to the next station on the "Railroad"—the home of a Quaker storekeeper on the outskirts of Cambridge village. If the colt could stand the journey Bill hoped to reach the place that night. He pushed ahead steadily throughout the morning. Fortunately for his plans the day turned cloudy and cool before they had gone far. A few drops of rain fell, laying the dust, and there was no sun to beat oppressively down on the travelers.

At noon Bill looked carefully behind him down the long winding road. A distant farm wagon was the only thing in sight, and he led his cavalcade into a thicket of leafy brush that would hide them from any passing eye. He had chosen the place not only for its cover but because a small stream, crossing the road under a culvert, promised water. They were a hundred yards into the woods before he stopped. For safety's sake he tied Jody to a tree. Then he unloaded the sack from the mare's back and undid the fastenings at the end nearest the colored boy's head.

"Banjo," he said, when the little Negro's frightened eyes appeared, "I'd like to let you get out an' walk around, but I don't dare. This thing is packed just right, and I mightn't be able to get you covered so well another time. Here's a drink o' water an' I'll bring you some grub in a minute."

They rested there for a good hour. The morning's march of a dozen miles seemed to have done little Bub no harm, but he was content to lie quietly in the grass while his mother grazed close by.

When Bill decided it must be one o'clock he got up and rearranged the ears of green corn in the end of the sack. "Next time I open this," he told the young runaway, "I reckon you'll be safe in Cambridge an' out o' my hands. But you've still got a long ride ahead o' you." He tied the bag firmly and swung it up to its place across the mare's back, lashing it on as before. A scouting trip to the edge of the thicket revealed no passing travelers, and Bill led his charges out on the road again.

The miles stretched out endlessly through that gray afternoon. Bill's own legs grew tired, for it had been months since he had attempted such a long day's journey. The mare never slacked her plodding gait but her foal was obviously weary by late afternoon. With five or six miles still to go, Bill took a chance on another hour's rest.

He found the young Negro's face drawn and gray when he opened the sack. "Ah ain't feel so good," the boy panted. "Seem lak de stummick gwine jolt out o' me ev'y step."

Bill lifted Banjo's head and offered him water from the dipper, but the youngster could not drink. "Dat ridin' all double-up done make me dizzy," he whispered, rolling bloodshot eyes.

Here was a situation that had Bill worried. There was nothing for it but to get the boy out of the sack and see if walking would revive him. He made certain first that their hiding place in the woods was wholly concealed from the road. When he pulled Banjo free the colored boy was too weak to stand, and it took five minutes of rubbing and slapping at his legs to start the circulation. Meanwhile Bill kept up a whispered conversation that was as cheerful as he could make it.

"Now try, Banjo," he urged. "Come on, you can take hold o' my arm. There, that's better, isn't it?"

"Yassuh," the boy tried to grin. "Ah kin stan' up, an' ma insides feels bettah. But yo' ain' gwine stick me back in dat bag, is yo'?"

"No," said Bill. "You're going to walk the rest o' the way, but we've got to wait till dark to do it."

They stayed there resting till the twilight deepened. Bill repacked the sack with corn and tied it on Martha's back once more. Then he told the small darky exactly what he had to do.

"Soon as we hear anybody coming," he said, "you duck into the brush or lie down back o' the nearest fence. An' you stay there till they've passed. I'll whistle like an owl when it's time to come out. Listen—like this." And he puckered his lips in a quavering screech-owl call.

It was late that night when they drew near Cambridge. Twice, along the road, the sound of approaching hoofs had sent Banjo scurrying into the bushes. But both times the riders who went by turned out to be ordinary farmers. After a long time they limped into the dooryard of a dark, silent house. Bill had recognized the place from Tobias Halsey's careful description. He left Banjo and the animals in the black shadow under the buckeye trees and went to knock on the front door.

At first there was no answer. Bill waited patiently, then knocked again, and at last a light appeared in an upstairs window. He saw a dim figure in a night-cap outlined by the candle's beam.

"Who's there?" asked a woman's voice, low and distinct.

Bill remembered the pass-word. "Package forwarded by William Penn," was his answer.

The head disappeared and he heard feet padding on the stairs. In a moment the door opened a few inches. There was no light, but he could see the white of the woman's night-dress behind the door-chain.

"Thee has him here?" she asked in a whisper.

"Yes. Back there under the trees. Want me to bring him in?"

"I would gladly take him," she hesitated, "but my husband was called away today. There is no one to carry him on."

Bill's heart sank. "We've had a bad time, Ma'am," he said. "He's only a young boy an' pretty well tuckered. They're after him sharp, too."

She seemed to be considering. "I have to be careful," she explained gently. "Thee didn't speak like a Friend, even though thee had the pass-word. But on the 'Railroad' we form sound judgments of people, and even though I haven't seen thy face I trust thee. There's a hiding-place at the back of the stable where thee and thy 'package' can stay overnight. Then the best I can do is give thee instructions as far as the next stop. Go back through the yard and Clara will meet thee at the kitchen door."

Five minutes later a plump colored woman was guiding the little troop through a passageway in the rear of the stable. There was room for the mare and colt at one end of the hidden chamber and beds of clean straw at the other. The Negress flashed her dark lantern on Banjo's face and clucked sympathetically.

"Mah lan'!" she said. "Yo' mighty peaked, po' lil boy! Jes' wait two jerks an' Ah'll fetch some milk an' cookies out yeah. Den y'all kin sleep an' sleep!"

MORNING light came in through the chinks of a burlap-hung window and roused Bill from heavy slumber. Banjo, already awake, was lying as still as a small brown mouse, only his white eyeballs moving. He ventured a grin when he saw Bill's eyes open, but he

268

NINETEEN

was too well disciplined to say anything.

The Yankee boy yawned and stretched his arms. "Looks like you feel better, youngster," he said. "Ready to travel again?"

"Yassuh," whispered the little Negro. "On'y Ah hopes Ah don' have to git in dat sack."

Bill chuckled. "Sort of a rough ride, I reckon, but it sure saved your hide yesterday. I wonder if they'll bring us breakfast."

He got up and went to the door of the passage-way, with an idea of finding some hay for the mare. But at that moment he heard a noise of hurrying feet outside. In three quick strides he reached Banjo and tossed handfuls of straw over him. Then he covered the boy with the sack of corn and stood waiting, his hand on Jody's muzzle.

From beyond the door came a panting sound and someone fumbled at the wooden catch. When it opened he saw the stout form of Clara, the colored woman. Her broad, good-natured face was puckered with lines of worry and she was still out of breath.

Carefully she closed the door behind her. "Dey's been yeah!" she gasped. "De man what use' to own dis chile, an' a marshal, too—axin' after runaway niggers!"

"Are they still here?" Bill whispered.

"No—dey rid off to town. Missus done tell 'em de trufe. She say she ain' seen no sign o' de slaves dey's lookin' fer. But dat man on de black hoss—

he don' look lak he satisfied. Ah knows y'all's hongry, but yo' better stay hid a spell. I'll bring some vittles quick as Ah kin."

She returned in a few minutes with a covered basket containing their breakfast. "Missus say she want to see yo', white boy," she told Bill. "Soon as yo's et, jes' slip out de back stable do' and meet her in de garden."

He found the Quaker lady waiting for him on a bench behind the high hedge. Seen in the daylight she was younger than he had expected—a frail, sweet-faced woman in her thirties, dressed in soft gray with a white linen kerchief at her throat. Her expression was calm and smiling.

"No doubt Clara has told thee," she said, after greeting him, "that we had visitors this morning. It seems the slave-catchers know that certain houses are not unfriendly to these poor people. They have gone on into the village for breakfast but they may return later.

"If my husband were at home he would find a way to send the boy on, but he had urgent business in Zanesville and may not be back before supper. The difficulty is that our 'package' must reach the canal at Newcomerstown tonight by ten o'clock. A certain canal-boat will be passing north at that time and, once aboard her, the lad will have safe passage to Cleveland.

"Does thee think thee could carry him that far? It's over twenty miles."

Bill thought it over. "We'd have to start right soon, Ma'am," he replied at length. "And in the day-time Banjo has to be kept out o' sight. Riding in that sack nigh cut him in two yesterday. That's what bothers me most."

"Poor lad!" she said. "Would it help, does thee think, if he had a pillow under him?"

"It might," Bill agreed. "We could put it right in the bag with him. What's the name o' this canal-boat I'm to meet?"

"She is called the *Susanna Jones*," the Quakeress answered. "Thee'll know her by two lanterns set on the top of the cabin. And thy pass-word will be the same thee used to me last night."

Within another half hour all their preparations were made. Somewhat dubiously the young Negro climbed into the hated sack and a plump pillow brought from the house was placed against his stomach. Then Bill carefully stuffed the ears of sweet corn in around him. When the bag was tied on the mare's back, Banjo admitted that he was much more comfortable than the day before.

The route had been explained to Bill. He would have a reasonably good road for perhaps half his journey. After that there was a stream to ford and the last ten miles were little better than a horse-track through the woods.

The cavalcade skirted the fields to avoid passing the tavern in Cambridge. But as they crossed the new National Road, a quarter of a mile to the west, the young peddler caught a distant glimpse of two horses—a black and a roan—tied to the hitching-rail in front of the inn. At least he knew the slave-catcher and his companion were not ahead, lying in wait for him.

It was another cool, cloudy morning. A good day for hard summer traveling. Bill urged Martha along at her best pace and was happy to see that the colt trotted beside her as fresh as ever after the night's rest. For a while the boy watched the road behind him, but there was no sign of mounted men.

He wanted if possible to reach his destination before dark, for much of the way would be rough going and through unknown country. So he pushed on without a pause till he saw the place where his trail turned off to the right, toward Wills Creek. It was an hour past noon then. He led the mare a short distance along the trail and stopped in a sheltered thicket to let the animals rest.

Banjo was standing the trip better than Bill had expected, thanks to the pillow's protection. He stayed in his sack and ate what was given to him without complaining. The lunch Clara had put up for their journey was a tempting one. There were cold fried chicken, beaten biscuits with butter and raspberry jam, and big slices of currant cake. Bill finished his meal and was about to return what was left of the food to his trunk when he noticed an envelope at the bottom of the little basket.

It was sealed, and the inscription was written in a dainty feminine hand. "Open this after thee has made delivery of thy package," Bill read. That was all it said.

He was tempted to tear the seal at once, but he

knew that the uncanny efficiency of the Underground Railroad was based on following instructions to the letter. There was some good reason, he was sure, why the message should wait. Wondering what it was all about he curbed his curiosity and put the envelope away in his inside jacket pocket.

Bill had loaded the heavy corn-sack across Martha's back and was just emerging from the clump of trees when he heard a quick pounding of hoofs coming along the main road. He waited, hidden by the brush, and in a moment the rider flashed across the gap at the foot of the side trail. He had a glimpse of a man in a gray cloak and hat, leaning far forward over his horse's withers. And the horse, flecked with foam but galloping eagerly, was the lovely black thoroughbred he had such good cause to remember.

The horseman did not even glance aside as he passed, but seemed intent on the road ahead.

"Bound for Coshocton," Bill mused. "Wonder what's taking him up that way. Well, thank goodness he's not on our track!"

They forded Wills Creek at the shallows where the trail came out of the woods, and struck on northward following a rough path over higher ground. There were a few scattered farms along the way, but most of the time they moved in the shadow of the forest.

The sun broke through the clouds after a while. Bill watched its steady descent into the west and quickened his stride. "Come on, old lady," he chided the mare. "Got to keep moving or we'll all be stumbling around in the dark before we get there."

It must have been about six when they scrambled down a wooded slope to the flats along the upper Muskingum. There was a road there, and many farms dotted the lowlands by the river. Bill whistled a tune to hide his nervousness and led his convoy out on the road. A little way off he saw a man coming his way, driving a pair of workhorses hitched to an empty wagon.

"Evening, mister," the boy hailed. "I'm strange to these parts. Maybe you could tell me the way to the nearest ferry."

The man stopped his team, stared at the packmare, the foal and the dog in turn, then glanced obliquely at Bill. He shifted his quid of tobacco and spat as if deliberating.

"Whar'bouts ye aimin' to git to?" he asked.

"I'm heading for Newcomerstown. That means I've got to cross the river an' the canal both, I reckon."

"Hm? Yeah, that's right. 'Bout a mile down this way ye'll come to a road north. Takes ye to Beeler's farm. He's got a flatboat'll take ye acrost if he ain't busy. T'other side ye kin foller the same road to the bridge over the canal, an' 'tain't fur then into Newcomerstown. Peddlin', are ye?"

"I was," Bill answered. "Sold all my goods now, an' going back north." He saw the man looking curiously at the big sack. "That's some sweet corn I got down below Cambridge," he added, and instantly regretted it.

"So?" said the farmer. "Mine ain't filled out yet. I could use a couple o' dozen ears."

"I'd like to let you have 'em," the boy stammered. "But—but I'm supposed to deliver the whole load. Thanks for telling me how to get there."

He started down the road and after a long moment heard the man cluck to his horses and move off. Then he breathed more freely. "How are you riding, Banjo?" he asked in a low voice.

"Ah's mekkin' out," the colored boy replied wearily. "But ain' we mos' dar, Mas' Bill?"

"It won't be much farther, I hope. You just hang on a while more and I'll take care o' you, boy."

They traversed the road to Beeler's farm and saw a big, bearded man coming up from the waterside toward the barn.

"Don't tell me *you* want to be ferried over, young feller!" the man roared ferociously. "Durned if it ain't as much as a feller's life's worth to git any chores done 'round here!"

Somewhat disturbed, Bill plodded on till he met the shouter face to face. Then he saw a good-humored twinkle in the little blue eyes and was relieved. "Sorry to be a bother," he replied, "but I would like to get across. I heard you ran some kind of a ferry here. What's the fare?"

The man scratched his beard and closed one eye to squint at the caravan. "Shillin' fer you an' three bits fer the hoss," he calculated. "We'll throw in the colt an' the dog rides free anyhow. Call it half a dollar."

The rate was high but Bill was in no position to quibble. He fished a silver piece out of his pocket and held it up for the ferry-man to see. "All

right," he nodded. "We're ready when you are."

Martha was hesitant about crossing the rickety gangplank, but with Bill tugging at her halter and the bearded man pushing behind, they persuaded her to step aboard. Once on the deck of the unwieldy craft she planted her feet far apart and looked up and down the stream with a fearful eye.

279

The river was not very wide at that point. A dozen violent shoves of the ferry-man's pole and they were drifting in to the landing on the northern bank.

"How far do you call it to Newcomerstown!" asked Bill as he paid the fare.

"Not above three mile," the man replied. " 'Tain't much of a place but it's on the main road from Coshocton to Salem an' New Philadelphy."

He looked as if he was about to ask a question regarding the corn-sack, but Bill bade him a hasty farewell and urged the mare up the hill through the gathering dusk.

Half an hour later the boy heard a familiar sound ahead. It was the long, lonesome hoot of a boater's horn on the canal. Old Martha pricked up her ears and shuffled forward as if she knew the end of their forced march was near. It had grown too dark for Bill to see more than the dim outline of the boat, but there were no lights on her cabin roof. If the *Susanna Jones* was moving on schedule he figured there would be at least two hours to wait before she made her appearance.

He turned off the road to the left at the bridge

and led the mare down to the towpath. There were trees fringing the canal. A hundred yards to the west he saw the dense shadow of a grove and guided his tired beasts toward it. In among the thick-growing saplings in the dark he fumbled for the pack-rope and released young Banjo from his burlap prison.

"Whe' is we, Mas' Bill!" the colored boy panted. "Still hidin'?"

"Yes," Bill whispered. "But it won't be much longer. There's a boat coming to take you, an' I reckon once you're on board you'll be safe. All we can do right now is stay quiet here and wait."

CHAPTER

BILL tethered the mare where she could get
a bite of grass and came back to Banjo's
side. "I don't dare build a fire," he told
him, "but there's some cold vittles left from noon.
You eat 'em. I'm not hungry yet."

The little Negro ate obediently and sat quiet for

282

TWENTY

a while. They could hear whippoorwills calling back in the woods. Jody sighed and stretched his nose on his tired paws. Then Banjo shifted to creep nearer, and Bill heard his whisper.

"Mas' Bill?"

"Yes, Banjo."

"Yo's been mighty good to me. Ah ain' never fergit it."

"Hush, boy. You've no call to thank me. An' we wouldn't have got this far if you hadn't done your part. I only hope you make it through to your folks in Canada."

The time dragged slowly. Bill was far too restless to be sleepy. Several times he got up and felt his way between the tree-trunks to the towpath. Overhead the stars were bright and a small breeze rippled their reflections in the water.

At last the listening boy heard a clink of trace chains in the distance. "There's a boat coming, Banjo," he said. "You stay here till I find out if it's the one we want."

From the edge of the grove he could see the bobbing silhouettes of the mules' ears and behind them the twinkle of a light—two lights!

The mules came plodding by. As they passed, one of them turned its head and snuffled, catching his scent. He stepped out on the towpath.

"Hello, there," he addressed the driver. "That the *Susanna Jones?*"

He could see the man jump. "Whoa up!" he

called to the team as he pulled on the reins. Then, in a guarded voice, "Who's there? Yeah—this is the *Susanna Jones*. What d'you want?"

Bill walked nearer. "I've got a package to go by her," he answered. "Is the captain on deck?"

"He's steerin'," replied the driver.

The momentum of the long craft brought it slowly abreast.

"What's wanted?" inquired a deep voice from the stern. And Bill repeated that he had a package to ship.

"Who from?" asked the captain.

"William Penn."

"Good. Bring it aboard."

In a few moments Bill had seen the young colored lad escorted safely down the companionway into the cabin, and the boat had glided off up the canal. As the stern passed under the bridge, he saw that the second lantern was gone from the afterhouse.

.   .   .   .

Back in the grove once more, Bill felt as if a heavy weight had been lifted from his shoulders. He was hungry, too. With no more need to hide his movements, he gathered a heap of dry wood close to the towpath, and kindled a fire to cook bacon and bannock and a cup of hot tea. And when the flames had died down he chuckled as he put two ears of his precious sweet corn among the hot coals to roast.

"If only I had some butter now," he said to himself, "I'd really have a feast!" That made him think of the empty lunch basket, and the basket, in turn, brought the letter to his mind. He went to his jacket pocket and got it out. His "package" had been delivered. It would be all right now to read the message.

Opening the envelope, he held the contents close to the embers of the fire. There were three crisp bank-notes—twenty-five dollars in all—and a slip of white paper. The words on it were in that same delicate hand-writing. All it said was: "In grateful appreciation of thy very helpful service."

"Gee!" he murmured. "I hope I'll be forgiven for saying the Quakers were tight!"

While there was still light enough coming from the fire he set about making his bed. It was useless looking for spruce tips or pine-needles in this hardwood country. But at least he could have the luxury of a real pillow! He had just pulled it out of the sack and was stuffing the corn back in place when Jody growled. Listening, Bill heard the thud of a horse's hoofs on the towpath.

The habit of caution was still upon him. Quickly he kicked dirt and rubbish over the fire and stepped back in the darkness among the trees. But the result of his action was just the opposite of what he had planned. Some dry leaves caught the flame, and as the horseman drew close a bright blaze illuminated the edge of the grove.

In the sudden light Bill saw a gleam on the satin skin of Cawley's black thoroughbred. The horse snorted and reared, then came to a stop under the firm hand of its rider.

"I wouldn't move if I was you," came the slave-catcher's easy drawl. "Fact is I've been lookin' fo' you all day. Put yo' hands up an' step out here."

Bill saw the firelight glint on a pistol barrel. With a cold feeling at the pit of his stomach he lifted his arms and walked out into the open.

Cawley threw a graceful leg over the cantle and dismounted, the pistol still in his hand. "You fooled me once," he said. "That's about as often as anybody can do it—an' stay healthy. Now, suh, if you don't mind, we'll just look over yo' outfit."

He strolled forward to the burlap sack and kicked it with his boot-toe. "Open it up," he commanded sharply.

Bill lifted the end which was still tied and shook out a cascade of green corn ears. When they lay exposed in an innocent heap he threw the empty bag on the ground.

The planter's dark eyes narrowed. "It was fuller than that yesterday," he snapped.

"That's right," said Bill. "I've got rid o' some of it along the way. An' there's two ears roasting in the fire—about ready to eat, I reckon."

Baffled, the southerner looked moodily at Bill for a moment. "So," he said, "you've got that blankety-blank little nigra hid in the woods here somewhere. Well, there's a cure fo' that. You pack up yo' mare an' move on out o' this—up the road to the next town."

Bill felt his temper slipping. "No," he said hotly. "I won't do it. The colt's clean tuckered out. If you still think I've got one of your Negroes—

which I haven't—you're welcome to look around. Or you can camp here all night for all I care. As for that pistol, you might's well put it away. This is a free country an' you can't go 'round shooting folks that are minding their own business."

Cawley stared at him, then tipped his head back in a hearty laugh. "Fancy that!" he chuckled. "A frozen-faced Yankee showin' fire, by George!"

He sobered then and Bill saw a flash of comprehension cross his dark, mobile face. He stepped back on the towpath and glanced up and down the canal. "Ah," he said. "I begin to see now. A very pretty scheme. Well, my young gamecock, I'll leave you to yo' roastin' years. If our trails cross again, I'll remember yo' dislike of firearms."

He swung nimbly into the saddle and waved his hand in farewell as the black horse galloped away up the towpath into the darkness.

Bill wondered how much the slave-catcher had guessed. He would overtake the *Susanna Jones* in half an hour at the rate he was traveling, but the canal-boat captain was probably an old hand at the business. The boy had a feeling that Banjo was safe.

The corn, as he expected, was charred in the flames and no longer fit to eat. Regretfully he kicked it into the fire, spread his blanket and lay down with his head on the pillow. As soon as he closed his eyes he was asleep.

.   .   .   .

Bill cooked a leisurely breakfast and gave the mare an hour or two to rest and graze, next morning. There was no longer any hurry. He had all the rest of the summer to get where he was going. And where *was* he going?

As he munched his johnnycake he pondered that question. The next county town to the northward was New Philadelphia. From there he could strike northwest on the road to New Lisbon and follow his old route back through 'York State. Or—and suddenly he knew that this was what he really wanted—he could head north along the canal to Cleveland.

"A little place called Buck Run." He could hear Mary Ann's voice saying those words, and see her coal-black hair—her flashing gray eyes—the proud lift of her chin. With sudden decision he jumped to his feet and rolled up his duffel. "Come on,

Jody—Martha—Bub," he called. "We're starting north."

He did not hurry on that journey, but neither did he lose any time. In Salem and New Philadelphia he sold his green corn and after that the mare carried the trunk. For the most part he followed the canal. At a place called Bolivar, which he reached the following day, he saw the *Susanna Jones* tied up at a dock. The driver was sitting on the gunwale, forward, whittling out a new whip-stock.

"Howdy," said Bill, strolling over to his side. "Maybe you don't remember me. Have any trouble with that package I put aboard—down by New-comerstown?"

The man squinted up at him and grinned. "So you're the lad, are ye?" he exclaimed. "Yeah, reckon I'd know ye by yer voice. Trouble? Well, we might ha' had, but the cap'n was too smart. Fixed the little feller up in a night-cap, an' put him to bed in a bunk with curtains. 'Bout midnight a Virginia man comes ridin' up an' orders us to stop. Skipper lets him search the stable an' cargo hold, treatin' him polite as ye please till he starts to open them curtains on the bunk in the cabin. Then he holds up his hand. 'Sir,' he says, 'ye wouldn't disturb my wife's privacy, I hope?' An' the slave-catcher bows an' backs away. 'Twas a beautiful thing to see."

He paused to bite off a chew of tobacco. "We passed the darky on up the line this mornin' 'fore daylight. Reckon he's most to Massillon by now."

At the leisurely pace Bill was making, he did not reach Massillon himself till early the second day after this encounter. There seemed to be a good deal of bustle in the place. Chaises, gigs and men on horseback raised a dust in the main thoroughfare, and Bill saw some of the business houses dropping their shutters as if closing for the day.

"What is it—a holiday?" he asked a young man in a butcher's apron.

"Nope. Hoss-trots over to Canton. Everybody's goin', I reckon. There—look! That's one o' the riders now. Man name of Merrick from some place East. He's leadin' his trotter back o' the gig."

Bill had already recognized the horse. "Yea, Tomahawk!" he yelled and waved his battered old hat.

The man in the gig pulled up short, staring not at Bill but at Bub, the colt. "Say, youngster," he called. "Who owns that foal?"

"I do," the boy answered in surprise. He led the mare over to the wheel of the gig and Bub skipped along beside her. "I got old Martha, here, at an auction, an' she dropped the foal last May."

Merrick seemed excited. He handed the reins to the man beside him and jumped out. First he looked at the colt, then at Martha. "That's it!" he exclaimed. "I remember that mare. A crazy horse-trader named Peel wanted to breed her to the Chief, but he didn't have enough cash. I gave him Tomahawk instead. I'd swear that's Tomahawk's first foal! And marked just like him. Look at that star and those white stockings! Listen, boy, I've got to get to the races, but what'll you take for the foal?"

Bill shook his head.

"A hundred dollars just as he stands? Make it a hundred and a quarter!"

"No," said Bill. "I reckon you mean it, Mr. Merrick. But I'm not selling Bub. Only time I ever saw Tomahawk trot, I said I'd rather own a horse like that than a million dollars. An'—well—I guess I've got one like him now!"

The sportsman looked at him shrewdly for a minute, then grinned! "Don't know as I blame you, son," he said. "But keep in touch with me. Let me know how he comes on. Here's my card."

He climbed nimbly over the wheel and took the reins. As the gig set off in a swirl of dust, Bill watched Tomahawk's clean legs flash into a long, easy trot. Then he looked down unbelievingly at the square of pasteboard in his hand.

"Gosh!" he said to the butcher. "Did you hear him? I've got a son o' Tomahawk!" And still walking on air, he led his cavalcade out of town on the road north.

.   .   .   .

At Portage and again at Akron, Bill asked the way to Buck Run. Some of the natives had heard of the place, but the directions they offered him were vague. It was not until he stopped one morning at a little cross-roads store near the Cuyahoga County line that he got definite information.

"Buck Run?" the storekeeper repeated. "Sure— 'tain't more'n six or eight mile from here, right

out that road yonder. Feller name o' Tom Ford
runs the gristmill there. What's that ye say ye
want—a hair-cut? Well, ye do sort o' need one.
I ain't no barber, but I reckon I kin oblige."

Half an hour later, with his long locks cropped
evenly above his collar and his clothes brushed to
some semblance of neatness, Bill set out up the side
road that led to Buck Run. He had a feeling, as
he marched along, that he was nearing the end of a
long journey. It seemed queer to him that he should
have no wish to go back to his old home. And yet
he knew there wasn't much for him there. A dreary
job making flannel, perhaps, and board with Wash
and Jenny, who didn't need him.

But Ohio was different. This big, sprawling, fer-
tile land had been good to him. With a certain
pride he considered the assets he had accumulated
since that April morning when he started. In cash,
counting the profits on his peddling, his haying
wages and the money he had received for carrying
Banjo, he had seventy-six dollars in his pocket.
Beaver-skins, as he had found by judicious questioning, were bringing four dollars or better in
Cleveland. With seven of them to sell, he could

count on another thirty dollars. And he owned a good, sound mare, a trotting-bred colt and a devoted hound-dog—all beyond price. That wasn't the end, either. He had his youth and his strength, hard muscles and a clear head. With these and nothing more a young man could go a long way in this new country.

Bill came over a hill and saw a stream running in a rocky bed through the sheltered green valley below. A little cluster of white houses stood among trees where the river broadened in a mill-pond. A shrilling of crickets and katydids pulsed through the warm noon, but as he descended the hill he heard another sound above their clamor. It was a girl's voice calling from a cottage door. "Yo-o-o, Tom—din-ner!"

He saw her standing on the step, wiping her hands on her apron. Then, before he could be sure, she flashed out of sight. Bill felt somehow weak in the knees, and his breath caught queerly. Funny what the look of a black-haired girl could do to a man! He trudged on. And before he reached the house she came out to meet him.

There was a blaze of color in her cheeks and the

dancing light in her eyes was more glad than mischievous. "Well, Bill," she said, "you—you did come, after all."

Suddenly he was bashful. "Yeah," he answered, kicking at the dust with a worn boot-toe. "I headed south a ways, first. Guess I should have written an' told you after I got my clothes back."

Mary Ann ran past him with a sudden cry. "A colt! Oh, it's darling, Bill! Is it Martha's?"

Bill told her the story as they went back to the barn and stabled the mare. "Did I hear you holler something about dinner?" he asked.

"Land, yes! I'd clean forgotten. And I didn't finish setting a place for you. I must go tell Sue. There's the basin right by the pump if you want to wash. Tom—that's Tom Ford, Sue's husband— he'll be coming up from the gristmill in a minute. Make yourself acquainted. Tom won't be here this afternoon," she added. "He's short-handed at the mill and he's going off to try to get a man."

Bill, bent above the wash-basin, grinned as she skipped up the back steps. "No, he's not!" he called after her. "He's got him a man right now!"

THE END